DANGEROUS
DECEPTION

Further Titles by Anthea Fraser from Severn House

BREATH OF BRIMSTONE
THE MACBETH PROPHECY
MOTIVE FOR MURDER
PRESENCE OF MIND

DANGEROUS DECEPTION

Anthea Fraser

This first world edition published in Great Britain 1998 by
SEVERN HOUSE PUBLISHERS LTD of
9–15 High Street, Sutton, Surrey SM1 1DF.
This title first published in the U.S.A. 1998 by
SEVERN HOUSE PUBLISHERS INC of
595 Madison Avenue, New York, N.Y. 10022.

British Library Cataloguing in Publication Data

Fraser, Anthea, 1930-
   Dangerous deception
   1.   Art thefts – Fiction
   2.   Thrillers
   I.   Title
   823.9'14 [F]

   ISBN 0 7278 5318 X

Typeset by Palimpsest Book Production Ltd,
Polmont, Stirlingshire, Scotland.
Printed and bound in Great Britain by
MPG Books Ltd, Bodmin, Cornwall.

Chapter One

'Now spurs the lated traveller apace
To gain the timely inn;'

Shakespeare: *Macbeth*

I HAVE often marvelled that so small a thing as a bee was responsible for everything that happened.

But as I was approaching the M4/M5 junction, where I'd planned to turn off for my proposed stay in Somerset, a large bumble flew through the open car window and started circling round my head. By the time I'd directed it outside again, I realised to my frustration that the junction was past and I was heading for Wales.

Resignedly I surveyed the options open to me; either I could turn off on the next A road and join the M5 further south, or I could totally revise my plans, stay on the M4 and see where it led me.

It made little difference; I'd not booked in anywhere and no one was expecting me. In fact, I hadn't wanted to come away at all, and it was only at my uncle's insistence that I'd finally set out.

I decided flippantly that if the registration of the next car I passed contained the letter S, I'd take the A road; if not, I'd continue the way I was going.

It didn't. Abandoning Somerset without a second thought, I headed into Wales.

This would be my first visit, though Uncle and Philip had

spent a holiday there some years ago. I remembered them talking about the peace and beauty of the area; it might be worth trying to track down where they'd stayed – a country hotel, up some valley beyond Cardiff.

Glad to have a firm destination in mind, I pulled in to the next service station and extracted my road atlas from the boot. With luck, one of the place names in the vicinity might ring a bell.

I found it almost at once: Dryffyd. *You take the Dryffyd road just past Cardiff*, Uncle had told my parents. I remembered it because it rhymed with 'triffid', and I'd been reading John Wyndham's book at the time.

I closed the atlas with a satisfied little pat, tossed it on to the back seat, and started off again. No warning bells rang in my head. All I remember thinking was that Uncle would be surprised when he received my postcard.

Two hours later, it was with considerable relief that I saw the sign 'Plas Dinas Hotel' and turned off the long, dusty valley road. This was the first hotel I'd come to, and whether or not it was the one I was looking for, I was more than ready for a break from my brooding.

For I'd been thinking, almost all the way, about Philip, and the main point of driving across the breadth of England and over the Welsh border had been to forget the whole, miserable business. It wasn't even, I told myself impatiently as I got out of the car, as if I had loved him.

The early September sun burned down, igniting the stone walls into a dazzling whiteness that hurt the eyes. The front door stood open, and I went thankfully inside.

It was dim and cool after the glare outdoors but, as my eyes accustomed themselves, I found myself in a pleasant foyer with a bar in one corner and a staircase rising from the centre. Somewhere out of sight an electric fan whirred busily, stirring the lazy air into a welcome draught.

"Good afternoon, miss. Can I help you?"

A girl detached herself from the shadows at the back of the hall.

Hot and thirsty, I decided to satisfy immediate needs before inquiring about accommodation. "I'd love some tea, if that's possible."

"Of course; will you have it in the garden? There are umbrellas—"

I shook my head. "No thanks, I've had enough sun for the moment."

"I'll bring it to the lounge, then." She nodded towards the room on the left of the hall.

"Thank you. And is there somewhere I can freshen up?"

"The cloakrooms are down that passage by the stairs."

"Bronwen!" A head appeared between some double doors behind her. "What did you do with the pile of clean napkins, then?"

I pushed open the cloakroom door and it swung to behind me, shutting off the sound of their lilting voices. It was a relief to wash away some of the strain of the journey. I splashed cold water on my face and patted it dry on the soft towel. No need, here, for make-up – a touch of lipstick was all that was called for. Not for the first time, I thanked Providence for the blessing of soot-black brows and lashes despite my ash-blonde hair. All that needed camouflage were the shadows under my eyes, and I told myself firmly that ten days of rest and country air would do more for them than all the beauty creams in the world.

The room indicated as the lounge was small and cheerful, its paned windows open to any available breeze, though there was no one here to take advantage of it. A copper jug full of poppies stood on the hearth, their glowing colours vivid against the grey stone, and above the fireplace hung a large watercolour – a peaceful scene of hills and valleys. Local, no doubt, I thought, admiring the sweep of cloud-filled sky.

I settled myself in a chair, grateful for the comfort of it after hours of jolting about in the car. I was more tired than I'd realised, and my half-formed decision crystallised. It was pointless to go any farther; even if this wasn't the right hotel – and there was no way of knowing – it was a pleasant, friendly

3

little place, and I was already beginning to unwind. The homely atmosphere would surely help me snap out of my depression.

Bronwen came in with the tray and I said impulsively, "Could you put me up for a while? I'm hoping to spend—"

My voice tailed off as her face clouded. "Oh, there's sorry I am, miss, but we've no vacancies. Only six rooms we have, and all of them taken."

"Oh." Having made my decision, I was acutely disappointed. "Well, it can't be helped. I was trying to find an hotel where my uncle stayed, but I've had more than enough driving for today."

"There's the Carreg Coed, just up the road. It's bigger than we are, they might have room."

I hesitated. I'd have to find somewhere for the night, and this could as easily be the hotel I was looking for. "Is it far?"

"Not above five miles. Shall I ring and see if they've any vacancies?"

"That would be a help; thanks."

As she went out, I turned with belated misgivings to the table in front of me. I'd expected a pot of tea with perhaps some biscuits, but here were warm Welsh cakes with unsalted butter, home-made jam, and slices of crusty currant bread. Out of the habit of enjoying food, I embarked on it half-heartedly, and was surprised to find how quickly I finished it.

I poured a second cup of tea, deliberately postponing my return to the hot car. Well, Uncle Matt, I thought, I've done what you asked. Now what?

"You should get away for a while, Clare," he had said, frowning worriedly at me. "All this business has taken a lot out of you."

"I'm all right," I'd replied a little waspishly. "Anyway, all my friends have had their holidays, and it's not much fun going alone."

"I'd come with you myself, but unfortunately I can't get away at the moment."

Which was as well, I'd reflected, because if he had, far from

4

forgetting the matter, it would have totally enveloped me. For Matthew was himself at the heart of it – he and Philip.

I took a quick sip of tea. Philip again. I couldn't get him out of my head today – probably because for the first time I'd had no work to occupy me.

Slowly I replaced the cup. A little therapy seemed called for; if I could steel myself to go back to the beginning, perhaps I'd see everything in perspective and, firmly ruling a line under the past, could forget it and get on with my life.

So, as 'the beginning' stretched back as far as I could remember, I let my mind drift to what, in memory, were the perpetually sunny days of childhood, the picnics, the treats and the holidays. And Matthew had always been a part of them.

From the start there was a special relationship between us, since in addition to being my mother's twin he was also my god-father. And though he'd had plenty of friends, he seemed to enjoy coming to our house, where he'd submit to joining in my games and reading me stories. In short, he was like a second father to me.

Then, just after my fifth birthday and when he was in his late thirties, he married a widow six years older than himself, with a twelve-year-old son. Shock had reverberated through the family.

"He could have had anyone!" I heard my mother exclaim hysterically, when she thought I was in bed. "What is he thinking of, saddling himself not only with that pasty-faced woman but her child as well?"

"It's called love, darling," my father had replied mildly.

I remembered standing on the stairs in my nightdress, one bare foot on top of the other as my world rocked about me. For how could Uncle love anyone but us?

As it happened, Aunt Margot won us over at once. She was a gentle, sweet-faced woman, and since she clearly adored Matthew, she was soon welcomed into the family.

Her son, at least in my eyes, was a different matter; I bitterly

5

resented having to share my uncle's affection with another child, the more so since Philip himself appeared to reject it.

Imprinted on my memory from that time was a tea-party at Conningley, when Aunt Margot had casually said, "Pass this to your father, Philip," and the boy had drawn himself up and answered clearly, "My *father* is dead."

In fact, throughout all those early years I never heard him call my uncle by any name that implied relationship, and as soon as he was eighteen, he addressed him as Matthew. Recalling this for the first time in years, it seemed ominously significant.

After the marriage, we inevitably saw less of them. Matthew and his wife sometimes had Sunday lunch with us, but Philip was by then away at boarding school. When the two of us did meet, there was still a faint animosity between us – on his side, perhaps, simply because I was a girl, but on my own due to lingering jealousy.

So our paths seldom crossed until the summer of six years ago. Philip had just left university and was about to join the family business when Aunt Margot died suddenly of pneumonia. The memory of those days was still painful – Matthew disappearing for long stretches to walk until he was exhausted; Philip, white-faced, abruptly leaving the dinner table; my mother in tears over the dishes.

But at least, with them spending so much time with us, the tragedy brought us close again, and a result of this was that Philip and I necessarily became more tolerant of each other.

However, I still regarded him as 'only Philip' until one day, Cora Browne – I haven't thought of her in years! – called round while he was there and pierced my unawareness with her blushes and giggles.

"Clare!" she whispered. "He's gorgeous! Where have you been hiding him?"

"Philip?" I had said in astonishment. "Gorgeous?"

Suddenly, looking at him with her eyes, I saw that perhaps he was, and it wasn't long before I began – quite shamelessly, it seemed now – to make use of him. If at any time I found myself without a partner – for a tennis match, a party, even to go to the cinema – I'd ask Philip to take me. Surprisingly, he always complied, and although I'd no particular feelings towards him, I enjoyed having him as an escort.

Philip's interest in me developed so slowly as to be for a long time unnoticeable. When, instead of waiting for my phone calls, he began inviting me out unprompted, I scarcely noticed the difference; and although we were spending more time together I attached no importance to the fact, ignoring the meaningful glances which passed between Matthew and my parents.

No one rushed us; we drifted along together and, because we were now coupled in the minds of our friends, no one else made a counterclaim. Philip's kisses never lit fires inside me, but they were acceptable enough, and he always stopped when I asked him. Obviously those wild, impassioned affairs I'd read about happened only in books. I was content, and the families were overjoyed. The only formality of our engagement was buying the ring.

My fingers had been unconsciously pulling and tearing at the paper napkin and it now lay shredded in my lap. I stared down at it. Was I after all ready yet, detached enough, to go back over everything?

There was a tap on the door and Bronwen came in. "Is there anything else I can get you, miss?"

I wrenched my thoughts back to the present. "No, no thank you. That was delicious. Did you get through to the hotel?"

"Yes, they have a room free, and they're expecting you. The Carreg Coed it is – you can't miss it."

"Thank you." At least I'd have a bed for tonight.

The sun was lying in wait for me, a suffocating gold dust in the car park. Reluctantly I turned the car out on to the road again. My departure from home that morning seemed light-years away.

I pictured the bleak little flat, empty and waiting. This was the time I arrived back in the evening, and I knew exactly how it would be looking, even to the slant of sunlight which fell across the sideboard.

Suddenly, stupidly, I was overcome by a wave of home-sickness for it, lonely as it was. At least I didn't have to pretend there. I wished vehemently that I'd not allowed myself to be persuaded into taking this holiday.

But it was too late for second thoughts. I straightened my back against the driving-seat and concentrated on the road ahead.

I heard the motor-bike before I saw it, a tiny speck in my driving mirror that grew rapidly bigger. Moving over slightly, I waited for it to pass, but to my alarm the rider slowed down as he reached me and waved at me to stop.

Horror stories of deranged attackers flooded my mind, and my foot was already on the accelerator when, to my untold relief, I recognised the waiter from the hotel I'd just left.

"Glad I managed to catch you, miss," he said breathlessly. "It's Gareth, from the Plas Dinas. There's a message just come for you."

He handed me a slip of paper.

"For me?" I said blankly. "But it can't be – no one knows where I am."

"Well, see, a gentleman phoned from London. Wanted to speak to a Miss – Lawrence, is it?"

"Laurie?"

"That's it. Said you were calling in for tea and he'd hoped to catch you – a fair-haired young lady on her own." His shrug was self-explanatory. "Queer message it is, and all. Couldn't make sense of it myself, but he said it's to do with a treasure-hunt. Made me read it back to him, word for word."

I glanced at the paper in my hand, and if the gods of chance were holding their breath, nothing warned me of the fact.

Aladdin delayed, I read in an unformed scrawl, *but Beanstalk still on schedule. Sinbad will make contact. Jack.*

"I'm not surprised you couldn't make sense of it," I remarked, "but I can assure you it's not for me. As I told you, no one knows where I am. What else did this mysterious caller say?"

"Wanted to know if you'd left for the Carreg Coed. I asked Bronwen and she said you had."

"Curiouser and curiouser. Well, thanks, Gareth, but I'm no wiser than you are. Sorry you had a wasted journey. Have a drink on me when you get back."

"Oh, I couldn't do that miss, specially if it's not for you after all."

I smiled. "Then put it towards a night out with Bronwen!"

He grinned delightedly. "That obvious, is it? Well, thank you, miss, and sorry to have troubled you."

The slip of paper had dropped to my lap and I hastily held it out, but he was already revving up his bike, and with a raised hand roared past me back down the road to the Plas Dinas.

I re-read the message, hoping that the treasure-hunt could proceed without it. Then, with a shrug, I slipped it into my bag and started the car again.

It was only a few minutes later that I came to a side road on the left, with a notice-board proclaiming *Carreg Coed Hotel 200 yards. Full Board, Morning Coffee, Lunches, Teas, Dinners*.

I turned the nose of the car on to the unmade private road and bumped gently along until I came to the hotel gateway on the right. The road ahead petered out into a footpath leading up the hill and as I turned into the gravelled drive I had my first sight of the Carreg Coed, a rambling stone building against a background of shrubs and rocks.

As Bronwen had said, it was altogether bigger than the modest little Plas Dinas and there were more signs of life about it. Two children played on the grass, bags of golf-clubs and fishing tackle were stacked in the porch, and on a tennis court behind the car park, a young couple were engaged in an energetic game. The sound of their voices came through the open car window.

It all looked much as I'd expected, a comfortable hotel catering to the tourist trade, and there was certainly no ripple of unease, not the faintest premonition that I was about to be catapulted into danger.

I parked the car and, with absolutely no thought of the consequences, went inside.

Chapter Two

'Pluck from the memory a rooted sorrow . . .'
                              Shakespeare: *Macbeth*

THE HALL, unlike that of the smaller hotel, was large and bright, the woodwork all painted white. There was a reception desk across from the door with what looked like an office behind it, and, on the counter, a visitors' book and a bell.

To the right, a glass wall separated the lounge from the rest of the hall. My quick glance took in a couple of old ladies and a man studying a map. I rang the bell, and almost immediately a pleasant-faced woman appeared from the office.

"Good afternoon. Can I help you?"

"I hope so; someone phoned from the Plas Dinas to reserve me a room."

"Ah yes." She pulled a book out from under the counter. "You're in luck, we've had two postponements today, both singles. The lady in number five won't be here till Sunday, which will give you two nights. If you decide to stay longer, I'm sure we can fit you in somewhere."

She raised her voice. "Evan!" A boy appeared at the office door. "Bring in the lady's case, would you, and take it to number five."

"The boot's open," I told the boy. "It's the blue Golf."

He nodded sullenly and went through the swing doors.

"Would you mind signing the visitors' book? We don't seem to have a note of your name."

11

"It's Laurie," I said, scrawling it, together with my address and the car registration number, in the appropriate columns.

She lifted the counter and came out into the hall. "I'll take you up. I'm Mrs Davies, by the way – my husband and I are the proprietors."

I followed her up the wide, shallow staircase which adjoined the glass wall of the lounge, self-consciously aware of the interested gaze of the old ladies. At the top she turned left, stopped at a door and unlocked it.

The room we entered was small but comfortable. There was tea-making equipment on a stand and its single bed was neatly covered with a green spread.

"Not many places have single rooms now," Mrs Davies remarked, following the direction of my eyes. "Being an older establishment we still have a few, and I can tell you they're in great demand." She smiled. "On the debit side, though, I'm afraid there's no *en suite* bathroom, but you'll find a couple at each end of the corridor."

She gave a quick, professional glance round the room and turned to go. "If there's anything you need, don't hesitate to ask. Dinner is served at seven."

There was a tap on the open door and the boy Evan came in with my case. He avoided my eye when I tipped him, and I found myself regretting the engaging Gareth and his Bronwen.

Then I was alone. Now what did I do? I wondered, with a feeling almost of panic. Nothing at all, for ten days? I'd be mad with boredom by the end of three!

Dispiritedly I started to unpack. Then I changed out of my creased blouse and skirt into a dressing-gown, settled myself on the wide window-seat, and determinedly opened the new paperback I'd brought with me.

The sun was hot on the back of my neck, and after a few pages I turned and sat gazing out across the little garden and, beyond, the dry grass and rocks and rising hills, to the blue wedge of sea.

Below me, the children were still playing with their ball, but an altercation had broken out. Voices were raised, then a wail of protest.

I only half heard them. My thoughts were slipping away again, the warmth and my physical tiredness relaxing the will-power that, for the last half-hour or so, had kept them away from Philip.

Our engagement had made little difference to our lives. I was in no hurry to marry and Philip didn't press me. The months passed uneventfully, and if I was aware of a small, nagging discontent occasionally, I pushed it to the back of my mind and refused to examine it.

Then, three weeks before my twenty-third birthday, disaster struck: my parents were killed in an air crash returning from holiday. My world teetered, rocked, shattered into fragments, and of course it was Matthew and Philip who picked up the pieces.

"You still have us, Clare," Matthew kept saying, those first dreadful weeks. I knew his grief almost equalled mine; he and my mother, as twins, had been very close, and it was to him I turned for comfort during the worst times. Once or twice, as his arms folded round me, I caught a glimpse of Philip's white, anguished face and felt a passing guilt.

They were both anxious to bring the wedding forward, to give me extra, much-needed security; but, perversely, it was then that I started to have serious doubts about my feelings for Philip.

After the tragedy I had moved temporarily to Conningley, where I found his constant presence an irritation – a reaction that filled me with panic. If only it could be just Uncle and me, I caught myself thinking more than once, and was appalled.

His unfailing good humour began to grate on raw nerves until I longed for him to disagree with me, to assert his own opinions once in a while. And when, as I came to do,

13

I automatically disagreed with everything he said, he'd merely smile and reply, "No doubt you're right, darling!"

At last I could stand it no longer, and after dinner one evening I braved Matthew in the library. "It's been sweet of you to have me here," I told him, "but I think it's time I stood on my own feet."

He looked up in consternation. "You're not going back to that empty house?"

"No, but I've seen a furnished flat advertised which sounds ideal. I—"

"But Clare, why? I hoped you'd be staying on here till the wedding."

I shifted uncomfortably. "It's just that Philip and I are rather on top of each other," I said. "I – need a bit of space."

"But we're out all day," he protested. "Anyway, I thought two people in love couldn't see enough of each other."

I bit my lip. "Please try to understand. You know how much you mean to me—"

"And Philip?"

"Of course," I said quickly, "but he wants me to settle on a wedding date and I'm not ready yet. Honestly, I think I'd be better away for a while."

"You must do as you think best," he said heavily, "but I admit I'm disappointed. Still, these things can't be hurried – take as long as you need."

So with his reluctant agreement and to Philip's obvious dismay, I moved to my flat and breathed more freely.

Slowly, life returned to what passed for normal. I still worked on the local newspaper and, telling myself it was what I wanted, spent most evenings alone in front of the television.

Philip phoned every day, though sometimes, guessing it would be him, I let it ring unanswered. Once, when he called at the flat, I stood watching him from behind a curtain and didn't let him in; and when I did see him, I increasingly turned away from his kisses, making excuses.

It was a difficult time in other ways, too. After discussions with Matthew and the family solicitor, I'd decided to put my old home on the market, which involved the heart-breaking task of going through my parents' things, sorting out which of the books, ornaments and furniture I'd known all my life would now have to be sold.

This was made even harder by the fact that the flat, convenient as it was, didn't feel like home and I couldn't settle in it. I wasn't sleeping well, and the doctor, approached in desperation, murmured platitudes about delayed shock. I was wondering just how much longer I would drift in this limbo when, out of a clear sky, the scandal broke.

My back went rigid against the warm wood of the window frame. Well, here we were, full circle, back to the point I'd been fighting to forget for the last three months.

Somewhere out on the hill a sheep bleated and was answered by another. The children had long since vanished inside. The first shadows were beginning to creep across the garden and, far above me, a silver microdot that was an aeroplane droned its way over the limitless sky. I drew a deep breath and let the memories come.

The first inkling I had of anything wrong was an early-morning phone call from Matthew, cancelling an invitation to lunch in town. He sounded strained.

"Something's come up which must be dealt with at once. Until it's sorted out, I shan't be very good company, my dear. I'll be in touch again soon."

And before I could question him, he rang off.

I was not unduly worried at this stage, but it did cross my mind that it was about ten days since I'd seen Philip, though my reaction to his absence had been only relief. I pushed my uneasiness aside and left for the office.

In the middle of the morning, Tom Bailey, one of our newer reporters, tapped on the door, his eyes gleaming with excitement.

15

"So you *have* come in today! Good for you! I never thought you would."

I looked up with a frown. "Of course I've come in; why shouldn't I?"

"Well, OK, so the story's not out yet, but you must know we have it and it'll be on the streets by lunch-time." He eyed me curiously. "Any chance of an inside angle, since you're here?"

"Tom, I've no idea what you're talking about. Now leave me alone; I've got work to do, even if you haven't."

To my annoyance, he hitched himself on to a corner of my desk. "Well, you're a cool customer, I'll give you that."

"Look, what is this?" I burst out irritably. "What are you getting at?"

"Oh, come on now! Family loyalty is one thing, but the nationals have it now, and we can get an exclusive slant if you'll play ball. After all, you're engaged to the guy."

My impatience was suddenly swallowed up in concern. I said urgently, "Tom, what is it? Has something happened to Philip?"

He looked up from the notebook he'd opened, his face a mask of amazement.

"You're not seriously telling me you don't know?"

"Know what? What *is* it, for pity's sake?"

He slipped off the desk, hastily pushing his notebook into his pocket. "God, Clare, I'm sorry. I'd no idea – I mean, I just naturally assumed – and when you seemed so cool about it, I thought there wouldn't be any harm—"

I stood up and leant over the desk. "Tom Bailey, if you don't stop beating about the bush I shall scream! Tell me everything you know, at once."

He was plainly embarrassed now. He cleared his throat.

"Well, of course nothing's actually been confirmed. There'll probably be an official denial any minute."

"Tom—" I began warningly.

He avoided my eyes. "Well, it seems there's been an almighty bust-up between Philip Hardy and his step-father."

16

"Bust-up?" I repeated stupidly.

"That's the story going round. The old man discovered some discrepancies somewhere and it looks as though Philip was responsible."

I said out of a dry mouth, "That just isn't possible."

"Look here, Clare," Tom said awkwardly, "let me at least verify it before I say any more."

"No, go on," I insisted, and my voice seemed to be coming from a long way away. "I don't believe it, but I want to know what's being said."

"Well, several things have come to light, but the climax was the business with these clients – antique dealers, I think. They're heavily insured with your uncle's firm, and Philip handles their account. They were broken into the other night, and some new pieces which hadn't been valued were taken. There seem to be grounds for believing Philip was the only one who knew they'd arrived and where they'd been stored."

"They're saying Philip *stole* them?" I couldn't take it in.

"No, not personally – that he sold the information to someone else. They've got hold of some character who insists he got the gen from him."

"But didn't he tell them all to go to hell?"

"It seems not. At first his step-father refused to believe it, but the story goes that when he asked Philip for an explanation, he flew off the handle and resigned from the firm."

I said slowly, "This is quite ludicrous."

"Yes – well, there it is. I'm sorry, Clare. If I'd realised you didn't know, I'd never have busted in like that."

"It's all right." My voice was quite steady. "Now, would you mind leaving?"

"Sure." He went quickly from the room.

With cold hands I pulled the telephone towards me, but it was a full ten minutes before the lines were clear to take my call, and even then I learned nothing.

"I'm sorry, neither Mr Bennett nor Mr Hardy is available

today," said the clipped voice of the switchboard. "I could put you through to their secretaries—"

"It doesn't matter."

I walked through the outer office with head high, aware of quickly stifled whispers as I passed. The streets were busy with mid-morning crowds, but I drove on auto-pilot, my mind seething with my conversation with Tom.

There must be some mistake. He'd misunderstood. There couldn't possibly be any truth in it.

Conningley lay basking in the June sunshine. I drew up at the door and walked straight in. Mrs Withers, the housekeeper, was in the hall, her eyes red-rimmed. I remembered for the first time in years that it was my mother who'd engaged her, when Aunt Margot died.

"Oh, Miss Clare—" she began, her voice breaking.

"Is Philip here?"

"He's in his room, but I don't—"

I walked past her and up the stairs, conscious of her staring after me. I tapped on Philip's door and, without waiting for an answer, went in.

He was at the far side of the room, putting things into a suitcase. He turned quickly, and I was shocked by his face. For the first time, I wondered if the rumours could be true. He stepped quickly towards me, but I didn't move.

"Clare!"

He stopped and for a moment we stared at each other. Then he gave an odd, lopsided little smile. "Well, Clare?"

I moistened my lips. "Is it true?"

"That I've left the firm? Yes."

"But Philip – why?"

He turned sharply away. "If you've heard so much, you must know the rest."

"But – it isn't true?" I was pleading more for Matthew's sake than my own.

He turned back to me. "Do *you* believe it?"

I stared into his burning eyes. At that point I honestly didn't know what I believed, but I'd hesitated too long. He gave a harsh laugh.

"So! *'Woman's faith and woman's trust'*!"

I whispered, "It will kill your father."

"He's not my father." A far-away echo, which at the time I didn't stop to pinpoint, underlined his conviction.

"But he's been like one to you," I said shakily. "All these years he's loved you, been proud of you—"

"All these years," he repeated bitterly, "I've bowed and scraped to him – yes sir, no sir, three bags full sir. No question of asking what *I* wanted to do. No matter if insurance bored me stiff, I was expected to comply with his wishes. Well, I've had it – and him – in a big way."

He looked at me challengingly. "Which leaves the million dollar question: what about you?"

I felt my mouth go dry. "Me?"

"Yes; who gets your vote, him or me?"

"You're asking me to – choose between you?" The words sounded stiff and melodramatic, but he didn't seem to notice. He was very still.

"I suppose I am."

Even in my dazed state, I was aware of the undercurrent in his voice. This wasn't the light-hearted, debonair Philip I knew. His face was stiff and cold but his eyes held mine with a desperate appeal that was more than I could bear.

"Please don't, Philip!"

He moved at last. "As I thought. He wins, hands down. Very well. In the circumstances, I can hardly expect you to share my disgrace." He forced a laugh. "I hereby release you from any commitment. Is that the right wording? Anyway, it's your cue, if you feel so inclined, to whip off your ring and hurl it at my feet."

I made one last, frantic attempt. "Philip, if we all talked it over, surely—"

"*No*, Clare. In any case, the sanctimonious old devil has ordered me out of the house."

19

That did it. I thought numbly, *If I loved him, I wouldn't be able to do this.*

Slowly I drew off my ring. He held out his hand. I dropped it on to his palm and stared down at my bare finger. The circle of white against the tan made it look as though the ring were still there.

Without a word, I turned and walked blindly from the room, down the stairs and past Mrs Withers, who still stood in the hall, out to the car.

That was the last time I saw Philip. Investigations were, I gathered, continuing, but as yet there was insufficient evidence to convict him. His solicitor was claiming the leak had been in the clients' own firm, though no one seemed to believe this. Opinion was overwhelmingly that he had been luckier than he deserved.

In the bewildering weeks that followed, no one at the paper mentioned the matter again and Tom took care to keep out of my way, though all he'd done was to bring forward the disclosure by a few hours.

Matthew, tight-lipped and grim, went about his business like an automaton. Yet through it all, he kept insisting that Philip needed me.

"Go to him, Clare," he urged, time and again. "I can manage, but he needs you more than ever."

I shook my head. "I'll never forgive him for what he's done to you."

"Whatever he's done, he still loves you."

"And I love you. You've always been a second father to me."

He stared at me hopelessly. Then he said very softly, "My God, what have we all done to each other?"

"He's – not coming back?"

"I don't see how he can."

"Then it's just the two of us," I said. Incredulously, I realised that this was what I had wanted.

*   *   *

My face was wet with tears, but I felt a bleak sense of triumph. I've done it, I thought, I've been back over the whole thing, from start to finish, and looked at it from a distance of three months. And I still didn't see what else I could have done.

I stood up and eased my stiff back. Now, if this enforced holiday was to do me any good at all, I must put it all out of my mind. And as good a way as any of starting the cure would be to have a leisurely bath before dinner – which unfortunately, I remembered, meant venturing down the corridor.

I gathered my things together and opened the door, and at the same moment the door opposite suddenly opened and I was face to face with one of the old ladies I'd seen in the lounge. She peered across at me and her face cleared.

"Ah, so you've arrived, my dear!"

"Yes," I acknowledged, a little doubtfully.

"Did you have a good journey?"

"The traffic wasn't too bad, but it was very hot."

"Yes, yes, it must have been."

She seemed to be waiting for something, so I said in explanation, "I'm just going along for a bath."

"Most wise – I'm sure it will refresh you."

And, as she still stood there, I added somewhat formally, "May I introduce myself – my name's Clare Laurie."

"Yes," she nodded amiably, "and I'm Miss Hettie. The younger one," she added mysteriously, and moved away towards the stairs.

I watched her go with a slight frown. Then I turned in the opposite direction in search of a bath.

Chapter Three

'The guests are met, the feast is set.'
       Coleridge: *The Rime of the Ancient Mariner*

I SAW the note as soon as I returned to the bedroom. It was propped against the dressing-table mirror, held in position by my hair-brush. For a moment I stood by the door staring across at it. Then I walked quickly over and picked it up.

Aladdin delayed, but Beanstalk still on schedule. Sinbad will make contact. Jack.

My first thought was that Gareth's note must have dropped out of my bag and someone – perhaps the chambermaid – had picked it up. But almost at once I realised that, although the message was identical, it was not in fact the same piece of paper. This was printed in neat block capitals.

Puzzled, I felt inside my bag. The first note was still there, so this one had a different origin. The caller, whoever he was, had asked Gareth if I were coming to Carreg Coed; it now seemed that, in case the waiter hadn't caught up with me, he'd taken the precaution of sending the message on ahead. Which meant that however incomprehensible it was to me, he must regard it as important.

Thoughtfully I tapped the note against the palm of my hand. Mrs Davies might know something about this second message; the best thing would be to hand it over to her, explaining it must be for someone else. That, surely, would be the end of the matter.

I started to get ready for dinner, selecting a sleeveless dress in hyacinth blue which, Philip had told me, exactly matched my eyes. But I didn't want to think about Philip. Picking up the note, I went downstairs.

There was no sign of Mrs Davies when I reached the hall, but a ginger-haired man was behind the desk. He looked up with a smile.

"Miss Laurie? Good evening, I'm Wynne Davies. Got everything you want?"

"Yes, thank you. Mr Davies, are there any motor-bike scrambles or treasure-hunts organised for this weekend?"

He looked surprised. "Not that I've heard of; why?"

"This message was waiting for me when I returned from my bath. There's obviously some mistake – it doesn't convey anything to me. I wondered if you could throw any light on it?"

He took it from me, and though his eyebrows lifted as he read it, he merely said, "Positively none, I'm afraid."

"I – suppose it must have come by phone?" I didn't see the point of mentioning the earlier one.

"I'll find out. Excuse me a minute."

He went through to the office and I caught the murmur of voices. Idly I turned the visitors' book round and my eyes flicked up the page. No new arrivals during the last week; everyone here must know each other by now.

The deep swishing of the swing doors behind me made me turn as a tall, good-looking man came into the hall. His face was tanned and he had the kind of large, loosely knit frame which looks its best in the casual clothes he now wore. As he came towards me, his eyes were frankly appraising, but he passed me with a formal enough "Good evening" and went on up the stairs.

At my elbow, Mr Davies said, "I'm sorry, Miss Laurie, I've no idea where this came from. None of the staff knows anything about it, and there haven't been any phone calls for the guests today."

He handed it back to me, and I unwillingly took it.

23

"Did you leave your door on the latch by any chance, when you went for your bath?"

"No," I said slowly, "I'm almost sure I didn't. I certainly had to use the key when I came back."

"That's what I don't understand, see; there are only two to each room, yours and the chambermaid's. And she's been sorting out the linen with my wife for the last hour."

The first prickle of unease crept up my spine as what I'd only subconsciously registered struck me for the first time: whoever had left the note had access to my room. And it hadn't been the chambermaid.

Wynne Davies was looking at me with a worried little frown. I made myself say lightly, "Well, there's no harm done. If anyone's expecting a message, perhaps you'd tell them I have it."

I turned away and, taking my courage in both hands, walked into the now crowded lounge.

I was hesitating just inside the door, feeling like a fish out of water, when someone came in behind me and a man's voice said cheerfully,

"Hello, have you just arrived?"

I turned gratefully. He'd an intelligent, rather bony face, short black hair cut *en brosse*, and was holding a whisky glass in his hand. I smiled back.

".Yes, and feeling very much the new girl! My name's Clare Laurie."

He held out his hand. "Morgan Rees. Perhaps a drink would break the ice? The cocktail lounge has been commandeered by a crowd of hikers, which is why we're taking refuge in here. What can I get you?"

"That's very kind. I'd like a dry sherry, please."

He put his head round the door and called, "Evan! Ask Dai to bring a dry sherry to the lounge, would you?"

He turned back to me. "Are you staying long?"

"I'm not sure; I have ten days' holiday but I might move on after a day or two."

24

"Well, let me introduce you to those near at hand. Most of us have progressed to first names by now, so may I call you Clare?"

"Of course."

He took my arm and led me to a pretty woman in her late thirties.

"Pauline, this is Clare Laurie – she's just arrived. Pauline Mortimer, Clare." We smiled and murmured.

Morgan Rees was continuing, "As I implied, there are exceptions to the camaraderie, such as our two schoolmarms over there. None of us would dare address *them* by their first names!"

He nodded to where two women sat chatting animatedly with a stout, bespectacled man. One – the elder, I judged – had short brown hair, unbecomingly fastened with a slide. Her face was innocent of make-up and she wore pebble-glass spectacles through which her eyes appeared microscopic. Her legs, heavily muscular, were planted four-square on the ground, and she wore a jumper of a singularly hideous shade of puce over a brown tweed skirt. Her companion was small and feathery, with an over-frilly blouse and dangling ear-rings.

The door from the hall opened to admit the barman with my sherry, followed by the man who had passed me in the hall. He came over to join us.

"My husband, Clive," Pauline Mortimer introduced. "Clive, this is our latest arrival, Clare Laurie."

His hand was large and warm and firm. "What brought you to this out of the way spot? Golf, walking, ancient monuments?"

I hesitated. "I'm not wild about any of them," I confessed. "It's just a rest I need, and plenty of fresh air."

"Well, there's no shortage of that."

"Talking of ancient monuments," Morgan Rees remarked, "where's our friend Harvey?"

The Mortimers glanced round the room. "He can't be back yet."

25

Rees turned to me. "Dick Harvey's steeped in archaeology. He's classics master at a boys' public school, and this is his one hobby. He comes here for his holiday every year and there can't be much of interest in the area that he hasn't unearthed by now."

The gong sounded in the hall and everyone moved towards the door.

"Do you know where the dining-room is?" Clive Mortimer was at my side. "Just beyond reception, on your right. Let me show you."

It was a pleasant room, whose wall of windows was filling it with the last of the evening sunshine. A waiter came forward to direct me to my small single table and Clive Mortimer released my arm. I turned from him with a smile of thanks and caught Morgan Rees's eye. He closed it slowly in a deliberate wink.

So Mr Mortimer's attentions were well known. He and his wife had moved to the only large table, over by the windows. It was now laid for two, but I guessed that the children I had seen playing made up the family. Everyone else had seated themselves around the room in ones or twos. The Carreg Coed was not, apparently, a family hotel.

My own seat was in line with the door, presenting a view diagonally across the hall to the swing doors, which, as I glanced at them, began to revolve wildly, shooting into the hall a small, dishevelled-looking man.

He stopped short on seeing the dining-room occupied, glanced at his watch to confirm his lateness, and, hastily smoothing down his hair, came straight in, taking his place at the table next to mine. There was an air of suppressed excitement about him which immediately caught my attention, and I examined him surreptitiously as he seated himself.

Slight in build, his dark hair receded from a broad forehead, but the large, spaniel-brown eyes had unexpectedly long lashes, which made them oddly appealing. His face – normally pale, I'd have thought – was flushed and, despite a quick wipe with his handkerchief, damp with sweat.

26

"Sorry, Harry," he smiled at the waiter, who was handing him a menu. "Lost all sense of time!"

"Gong's only just gone, sir."

"Good, good!" It was so obvious that he was bursting with news of some kind that the waiter dutifully led him.

"Have an interesting day, did you sir?"

"Harry, I can hardly believe it! Quite fantastic!" He literally rubbed his hands together. Then he caught me watching him, and his colour deepened still further.

"Forgive my exuberance, Miss—"

"Laurie," I supplied.

"—Miss Laurie, but I really did stumble on something today. Quite incredible!"

"How exciting," I murmured politely.

"Perhaps, if you're interested, I may tell you about it after dinner?"

I stifled a sigh, guessing that by this time the other guests were growing weary of his discoveries, and he would welcome a fresh ear. An evening lecture on the unearthing – if that was the word – of an ancient burial mound or whatever was not quite what I'd hoped for, but I hadn't the heart to discourage him.

"I'll look forward to it," I said.

He nodded, smiling, and, subsiding a little, turned his attention to his meal and I did the same.

"Table all right for you, Miss Laurie?" The waiter was beside me.

"Yes, thank you."

"Those near the windows are the most popular, of course, but we reserve them for the doubles. Perhaps when the gentleman joins you—"

I looked up. "Gentleman?"

"Yes, miss. Your friend. I believe he's been delayed?"

Was this, I wondered, the deliverer of the message? If so, I could hardly question him here. I said slowly, "I'm not expecting anyone."

27

For a second his eyes held mine. Then he smiled knowingly. "I understand. Beg your pardon, I'm sure, miss."

He moved away and I was left uncomfortably wondering whether 'Aladdin' was indeed expected, and if so, how he'd react when he arrived to find me here instead of whomever he was expecting. And again the faint wash of uneasiness lapped over me.

When I reached the lounge after dinner, the chairs had been turned companionably to face each other and a trolley bearing a coffee urn, cups and saucers stood in the middle of the room.

"Come and join us, Clare!" called Pauline Mortimer, and I was grateful to comply. Clive was handing round coffee cups as the smaller of the two school-teachers filled them from the urn. I wondered if Pauline knew of her husband's wandering eye, and pitied her.

"Have you met Dick Harvey?" she asked, as I sat down. "Clare Laurie, Dick."

He nodded and smiled shyly. "I rather forced myself on her in the dining-room, I'm afraid."

Pauline gave a spurt of laughter. "You, Dick, forcing yourself? I can't believe it!"

He flushed. "What I mean is, I was so excited I hardly knew what I was doing."

"And what had caused all this excitement?" asked Morgan Rees smilingly, standing over us with his cup and saucer.

"Well, you see, I came across something most extraordinary this afternoon – something which I should say is really valuable."

"'*The unsunned heaps of misers' treasure*', Mr Harvey?" boomed the muscular school-mistress.

"Not exactly, though it might be treasure-trove for all I know."

"Come on then, Dick." Clive, having served everyone, sat down on the arm of his wife's chair. "Now that you've whetted our appetites, you can spill the beans."

"Well, you see—" He stopped and looked suddenly uncomfortable. "Do you know, I think perhaps I'd better not say any more till I've had a chance to examine them again."

"Them? Dick, don't be so infuriating!" That from Pauline.

"No, really. In any case, I'll have to get in touch with the authorities—"

"*What* authorities?"

Quite suddenly he clammed up, and I knew we would get nothing more out of him. These meek, inoffensive little men can be remarkably stubborn when the mood takes them.

"Well, at least tell us where you've been?"

I turned my head at the unexpected American accent, and discovered it came from the stout man with glasses beside the school-teachers.

"I'm sorry." Bright pink now, Dick Harvey shook his head. He glanced round the room at the curious faces. "I really do apologise. I didn't mean to be so irritating, but on reflection I—"

"Relax, Dick," Clive said easily, "no one's twisting your arm."

General conversation resumed, and I found Morgan Rees beside me. "Are you beginning to sort us all out? It can be a bit daunting, I know."

I looked up at him. "I hadn't realised the gentleman over there was American. Is he with the school-mistresses?"

"No, his wife's in the corner there – the lady with the blue rinse. Mr and Mrs Zimmerman, from Chicago."

I glanced at the elderly lady chatting to the young couple who'd been playing tennis on my arrival.

"Isn't this rather off the beaten track for them?"

He shrugged. "They seem to be enjoying themselves, going on daily trips to places of interest. They're here for a few more days, then going on to 'do' Scotland."

"And the young couple?"

"Oh, they're our honeymooners. Rather endearing really, no

eyes for anyone else. Andrew and Cindy Dacombe. Call her 'Mrs Dacombe' and watch her blush!"

"I wouldn't be so unkind!" I glanced again at the girl. Her corn-gold hair was caught youthfully back in a ponytail and her short skirt revealed a pair of long, slender brown legs.

Her husband, who didn't seem much older, was snub-nosed, with red-brown hair that he'd obviously attempted to smooth down, but which nevertheless stood up in unruly spikes. I noticed that their hands were unobtrusively linked between their chairs.

Morgan said, "Anyone else I can fill you in on?"

"The old ladies?" They were sitting side by side on a sofa knitting industriously, both small and plump, with soft white hair twisted into buns at the backs of their heads. Alike as two peas, I thought. Even their clothes were identical.

"The Misses Jones – Olwen and Hettie. They keep pretty much to themselves."

I looked round the room. "And of course, the schoolteachers."

"Indeed. Norton and Bunting by name. Norton's all right, in a jolly-hockey-sticks sort of way, but Bunting looks as though she might die of fright if anyone said 'Boo!' to her."

"And this is the full complement of the hotel?"

"Apart from the Mortimer brats. There's one vacant room, but I believe it's booked. I heard Wynne Davies say the chap can't get here till tomorrow."

'Aladdin' again?

"And what about you, Morgan?" I asked, turning to him with a quick smile. "You've given me thumbnail sketches of everyone else – what do you do?"

"I'm a writer for my pains, strictly non-fiction. At the moment, I'm working on a biography of Owen P. Thomas." He glanced at me and laughed. "Go on, admit it – you've never heard of him!"

"Should I have done?"

"Not really; he was a Welsh politician during the last century."

"Why does he interest you?" I asked curiously, but before he could reply, Mr Zimmerman's voice reached us from across the room.

"Well, I admire you, Dick, I truly do. If you *have* struck gold, you sure deserve it, after all the slogging you've been doing, year in, year out."

"And so say all of us," Miss Norton confirmed. "You've earned your Aladdin's cave, Mr Harvey."

I jerked involuntarily and the coffee spoon rattled in the saucer I still held. Morgan took it from me and laid it down on the table.

Could the school-mistresses be responsible for the notes, I wondered incredulously, taking a leaf from children in their class?

No, that wouldn't work; it didn't take account of the man who'd phoned Plas Dinas. Then there was the waiter, who'd assumed I was here to meet someone. I shook my head to free it of the questions which suddenly filled it like a swarm of bees.

Across the room, one of the old ladies rose slowly to her feet and started to make her way towards the door. As she passed me her knitting bag slipped from her grasp, and as she fumbled to catch it, a ball of wool dropped out and rolled under my chair. I bent to retrieve it and handed it back to her.

"Thank you so much, Carol my dear. I may call you Carol, mayn't I?"

"Clare," I amended quietly. "Please do. Good-night, Miss Hettie."

"Olwen," she corrected in her turn. "I'm the elder one."

I looked after her as she went out, and turned back to find Morgan Rees laughing at me.

"The only way to tell them apart," he informed me, "is to look at the brooches they wear. Miss Hettie has a cameo and Miss Olwen an amethyst. At least, I think that's the right way

31

round. All this nonsense about the younger and the elder – they're twins, of course."

"How sweet that they still dress alike, at their age."

Talk became more sporadic and I felt my eyelids growing heavy. It had been a long day. Finally Morgan stood up and stretched. "I'm going outside for a breath of air – it's not ten o'clock yet. Anyone care to join me?"

No one responded and he laughed. "Lazy lot!" He looked down at me. "Perhaps you'll let me show you round in the morning, then? There are some lovely walks if you don't mind a spot of climbing, with spectacular views."

"Thanks, I'd enjoy that."

"Good-night, then. Pleasant dreams."

He left the room. Pauline was still talking to Dick Harvey and Clive had disappeared – probably to the bar. My eyes slid to the newly-weds, laughing softly together, and I felt a sudden twist of pain. There were obviously no doubts for them, their happiness was like a warm radiance.

I looked quickly away, and caught the curious gaze of the fluttery Miss Bunting. Embarrassed at being caught watching me, she bent her head lower over her crochet-work.

Suddenly, with a crawling sensation on my scalp, I knew I was still being watched, though less openly. My eyes darted swiftly round the room, but no one here was looking in my direction. I turned my head and my eyes were drawn up the glass wall to the staircase which rose alongside it. The lower steps were brightly lit from the hall and the lounge itself, but beyond the bend there were shadows and surely, as I looked, a pale smudge that could have been a face darted out of sight.

The hairs rose slowly on the back of my neck. Who was up there in the darkness, watching the brightly lit room below? And who in the lounge warranted such surreptitious spying?

I stood up suddenly, telling myself I was over-tired and imagining things. The sooner I was in bed, the better. Pauline looked round and I smiled apologetically.

"I think I'll go up now, if you'll excuse me. Good-night."

"Good-night, Clare. Sleep well."

The hall was deserted, but there was the sound of voices and laughter from the cocktail lounge. I leant over the reception desk, lifted my key off its peg and started up the stairs, my heart still thumping. Just short of the bend, I in my turn halted and turned to look down.

As I'd thought, standing here I could see the whole room below, like a television producer in his box high above the set – the Americans, the teachers, Pauline and Dick. And remembering his sudden reluctance to speak of his find, I wondered fancifully if some imaginary producer in his head had shouted "Cut!"

The thought had just formed when my heart suddenly lurched into my throat. Someone was coming down the stairs! I froze, telling myself I was in full view of anyone who chanced to look up, and therefore quite safe. Safe from what, I couldn't have said.

Had I been calmer, I'd have realised there was nothing furtive about the footsteps above me. In another moment, their owner had run lightly round the bend in the staircase and cannoned into me. It was Morgan Rees.

His hands caught and steadied me. "Clare, for goodness' sake! Did I hurt you?"

"I thought you'd gone out!" I said accusingly.

"I'm just on my way. I popped into the television lounge to watch the headlines, then remembered I'd left my sweater upstairs. Did you know we've a television lounge, by the way?"

"No." My heartbeats were gradually decreasing.

"Down there on the left of the entrance – on the opposite side to the cocktail lounge."

"It can't be very well patronised."

"No, most people want to get away from TV on holiday. Sometimes the Americans and the schoolmarms play bridge in there, if the lounge is occupied."

We stood awkwardly for a moment.

"Well—" we both said together – and laughed.

"Good-night again, then."

"Good-night, Morgan."

He stood to one side and I passed him and went on up the stairs.

I undressed slowly. I was tired, yet my brain was too active to allow me to relax and I was still unsettled by the unseen watcher. I switched on the bedside lamp, turned off the main light, and drew back the curtains.

Outside, all was dark and still. An owl hooted suddenly near at hand, making me jump. The room was still hot with the day's stored sunshine and I opened the window as wide as it would go and pulled the blankets off the bed. Then, with a little sigh, I climbed in, pulled the sheet over me, and began to read. It was about ten-thirty.

Chapter Four

'I have not slept one wink.'

Shakespeare: *Cymbeline*

I READ for a long time, hoping it would make me drowsy. It didn't, which was frustrating. I was determined to wean myself off the sleeping pills while I was away, and had no intention of giving in on the first night.

Footsteps and muted voices passed my door from time to time as the other guests came up to bed. Finally, I put my book down, turned off the lamp and resolutely lay down. But immediately, behind my closed eyelids, winding country lanes rushed past me, bends appeared and my body turned into them. Acknowledging that it was hopeless, I opened my eyes again.

After a minute they adjusted and I could make out the unfamiliar shapes of furniture, faintly visible in the light from the uncurtained window. I lay motionless, my head turned to the pale rectangle, watching the black ragged clouds skid over the sky.

And inevitably, my thoughts reverted to Matthew and Philip. Since that blistering hour before dinner, I'd been too occupied with my fellow guests to think of them, and I didn't want to start now. Safer by far to concentrate on Morgan and the Mortimers and the old ladies. Miss Hettie had the cameo, Miss Olwen the amethyst. Or was it the other way round?

An owl hooted again, and again I jumped. What was making me so nervy tonight? Admittedly there'd been one or two riddles during the last few hours, but they were puzzling rather than sinister.

Mentally I ran through them, in case any could account for my unease. The first, of course, was the note Gareth had brought me, with its childish references to Aladdin and Jack and the Beanstalk. Easy enough, at that point, to accept as a game of some kind – indeed, Gareth had said as much.

But the arrival of its duplicate gave it added significance, specially since there was no way to account for its presence in my room. Perhaps that was subconsciously causing my edginess.

More nebulous was that feeling, in the lounge, of being watched, and the glimpse of what I'd thought to be a face disappearing up the stairs. It could have been imagination, but it was directly responsible for my near panic when Morgan came innocently down the stairs. Really, I told myself severely, I was becoming neurotic.

The bar of brightness under the door disappeared as the light in the corridor was switched off. The hotel settled itself for the night. Still I lay there, willing myself to sleep with increasing desperation, and eventually, after what seemed aeons, I sank at last into the longed-for drifting between wakefulness and oblivion.

Then, from one second to the next, I was wide awake, lying rigid, heart pounding, eyes staring, wondering what had disturbed me. And in that moment it came again – a faint, metallic click.

My head swivelled to the door. Beyond the window, the clouds raced away from the moon and its pale light gleamed on the polished knob. And as I watched it, it moved.

I clutched the sheet tightly to my chin, staring with unblinking eyes at the slowly turning handle. When it had reached its full extent, the door creaked softly as pressure was put against it. Thank God I'd snipped down the lock. Two keys, Mr Davies had said, mine and the chambermaid's. Then who—?

After a timeless interval, the knob silently returned to its original position. Drenched in perspiration, my heart hammering, I waited, and my straining ears caught a faint rustling and scraping.

I sat up, scarcely breathing, in time to see a white oblong appear under the door. It was pushed farther into the room and another, less white, followed. Then there was a creak of the boards as my unknown visitor stole away.

My hand shot out for the lamp and the room sprang to life, reassuringly normal, with my clock on the bedside table and my clothes over the chair. But on the carpet just inside the door lay two envelopes, one white, one buff.

I gazed at them as though they might explode any minute. Then I was out of bed and at the window, my fingers fumbling with the catch as I closed it and pulled the curtains securely across. The airlessness would be stifling, but I would rather suffocate, I told myself grimly, than sleep with the window open tonight. There was a most convenient drainpipe just outside.

Cautiously I approached the envelopes and picked them up, feeling them between my fingers. The buff one was flat, with the flap casually tucked inside, but the white was quite bulky and had required some manoeuvring to ease under the door – the scraping sound I'd heard. There was, I saw now, a gap of at least an inch – one disadvantage of old buildings that Mrs Davies had omitted to point out.

Quite definitely I could not have received these by mistake; someone obviously thought it was I who should have them, and the explanation of a treasure-hunt was becoming progressively less convincing.

Useless to hand them in; the hotel staff had been unable to help with the note. But why should I be singled out? Was it a subtle attempt at harassment?

Suddenly anger replaced fear. What the hell did they think they were playing at, creeping about at dead of night and scaring the life out of me? I'd show them I could play games

37

too! I'd write a note from Goody Two Shoes and pin it on the hall notice-board. That should silence them!

I sat on the bed, ripped open the white envelope and pulled out a folded wad of paper. I don't know what I expected, but certainly not what I now held. It was a small booklet entitled *Cefn Fawr Castle* and on the front, scrawled in pencil, were the words *X marks the spot!*

Had I, after all, been too quick to dismiss the treasure-hunt? I opened it curiously. It was one of those pamphlets on sale at ancient monuments, full of references to the Great Hall, the Keep and the Norman Tower. At the back was a plan of the castle, with what appeared to be a long passage down one side, and almost at the end of this was a pencilled cross. Written faintly across the top of the page were the words *Rub out immediately*.

A folded sheet of paper had been slipped into the back of the booklet. I opened it and read:

Sweetheart: I'm passing this to Sinbad to await your arrival. By the time you read it, the full company should be there. Aladdin has directions to the loot, but needs your input as to location. Remember you're supposed to be lovers, but in public only – no shared room! You know the initial impact you have on people, so keep him in check and remember I've a very jealous nature! Seriously, darling, take care. We've worked so long for this. Shipment arranged according to plan. Burn this when you've read it. As always – 'Jack'.

I stared at it for a long time, while my anger ebbed away and panic spread its sticky tentacles over me. The game wasn't a game any more. I wished vehemently that I'd not opened the envelope. But I had and whoever had pushed it under my door – Sinbad, presumably, whoever he might be – would know that I had.

My fingers were shaking so much I had difficulty in

refolding the paper. I slipped it and the booklet back in the white envelope, and only then did I remember the buff one. Since the damage was done, I might as well open it, too.

It contained a single slip of paper, printed in the same hand as the note on my dressing-table.

How now, Goldilocks! it began breezily. *Glad to report Aladdin will be with us by lunch-time tomorrow. Operation Beanstalk scheduled for Tuesday – reconnaissance necessary Saturday or Sunday among holiday crowds. Can't disclose identity except in emergency – you know the rules! – but will be on hand if needed. Good luck! Over and out.*

'*Sinbad*'

Snippets of conversation flitted through my brain like crossed telephone wires: *The young lady won't be here till Sunday.* Evidently someone didn't know that. *When the gentleman joins you . . . The chap can't get here till tomorrow.*

So what could I make of it all? I wondered feverishly. It seemed a man and woman should have arrived here today, but had been independently delayed. Jack had phoned the Plas Dinas – where, perhaps, they'd arranged to meet and come on together? – to let her know 'Aladdin' had been held up, but was told she'd already left for Carreg Coed. So he'd phoned Sinbad – on his mobile, presumably, since the hotel knew nothing of the call. And Sinbad, not knowing the girl's arrival had also been postponed, assumed, like Gareth before him, that I was she.

But what lay behind it all? What did the cross on the plan of the castle signify, what was 'the loot', and what, in heaven's name, was 'Operation Beanstalk'? In a macabre way, the use of these nursery names made the whole affair more menacing.

My first basic instinct was flight. If I left straight after breakfast, with luck no one but the Davieses would miss me till lunch-time, and by then I could have got clear. But Sinbad, having delivered his message, might well be keeping an eye on me.

I had a terrifying vision of the little car racing for its life up the tortuous mountain roads, with Aladdin and Sinbad, in grotesque pantomime masks, hot on my heels.

Anyway, where could I run to? My name and address were in the hotel register – there was nowhere I could hide indefinitely.

Useless, now, to plead innocence. From whatever motive, I had opened the envelopes and seen the plan. I couldn't in any event appeal to Sinbad, because I didn't know who he was. For that matter, I couldn't trust *anyone* at the hotel, for if 'the full company' was gathered here, there was no saying how many were involved.

There remained the police, but what could I tell them? I didn't know anything, I had only a plan with a pencilled cross, and I could imagine official reaction to stories about Sinbad and Aladdin.

There was also still a very faint chance that the danger was imaginary; it *could* still be an elaborate scavenger-hunt, organised by a rambling club or some such, as Jack had told Gareth. In which case, I'd look very silly if I ran to the police about it.

The argument, rational though it might be, didn't convince me. Despite the closeness in the room, I was shivering with apprehension and it was imperative to steady myself so I could think clearly. A hot drink might help.

I flicked through the assorted packages of beverage on the stand, selected one containing chocolate powder and tipped it into a cup. Then I filled the kettle at the basin and, despite the proverb's warning, stood watching as it came to the boil, my mind going round and round this latest development. Was there anything of significance that I'd missed?

Yes! A sentence came back to me, offering a pinpoint of hope. Abandoning the kettle, I hurried back to the bed and opened Jack's letter again. *You know the initial impact you have.* Initial impact! Then Aladdin had never met Goldilocks!

Slowly a fantastic idea was forming. Could I – dare I bluff him into believing I really was her? Because otherwise, things might get very unpleasant. I had, after all, been handed what could be regarded as incriminating evidence, and even if I told him of the mix-up, he'd realise I knew too much.

If, on the other hand, I could go along with them until I learned what 'Operation Beanstalk' and 'the loot' were, I could present the police with the complete picture.

The sound of the kettle boiling merrily intruded on my brooding and I made my drink. Then, hands round the hot, soothing cup, I tried to marshal my thoughts.

On the plus side, Sinbad was already convinced of my identity; I could reel off a string of code names, and I had the plan. And Aladdin for his part would hardly be expecting a substitute.

The crux would come when the real Goldilocks arrived. When the expected approach wasn't made, she would contact Jack, who'd get on to Sinbad.

Well – I straightened my shoulders – if it came to that, I'd have to brazen it out – say I'd thought it was a joke. Blondes were supposed to be dumb, weren't they?

At best, I only had until Sunday; to have any chance of pulling off my deception, the proposed 'reconnaissance' must therefore take place tomorrow. After that, I should know exactly what was involved, and could decide my course of action. And with luck I could still be away before she arrived.

I glanced down at the letters. I was under orders to destroy them, but they and the notes were all I had to support my story and there was no way I was going to dispose of them.

Fumbling in my handbag, I took out the identical notes which had started the whole affair and slid them, together with the letters, into the buff envelope. Then, since I should later be showing the map to Aladdin, I obediently rubbed out

41

the pencil markings on it with the eraser on my diary pencil and slid it back into the white envelope.

Now to find a suitable hiding-place. Sipping my cocoa, I carefully studied the room. Then, setting down the cup, I dragged the dressing-stool over to the wardrobe, climbed on it, and, reaching up, explored the top with my fingers.

It was lined with sheets of newspaper, screened from below by the bevelled edge of the ornate frontage. Ideal, I thought, and climbed down to retrieve the envelopes, which I carefully inserted between the newspaper and the top of the wardrobe.

Feeling like a character in a spy novel, I replaced the stool and checked that no sign remained of my dead-of-night manoeuvres. Then, confident that I had done all I could for the moment, I climbed back into bed, switched off the light, and prepared to wait for the dawn.

Chapter Five

'Jack and Jill went up the hill . . .'

Nursery Rhyme

WHEN I opened heavy eyes the next morning it was as though I'd barely slept, though in fact I must have had four or five hours, since the hands of my clock pointed to seven-thirty. Breakfast, I'd been told, was from eight to nine.

Sighing, I reluctantly got out of bed and went to open the window. On the lawn beneath, the Mortimer children were again playing ball. There was the sound of a cow lowing, a sudden bleat from a sheep. In this normal, morning world, the night's adventures seemed absurd and unbelievable.

I turned from the window to make myself a cup of tea. Today, at lunch-time, Aladdin would be here, but in the morning sunshine I could feel no more than a tingle of anticipation. Surely my imagination had run away with me – there must be a simple explanation.

I washed in cold water in an effort to wake myself and, by the time the breakfast gong sounded, felt, despite my lack of sleep, ready for the day ahead.

As I emerged from my bedroom the honeymooners were approaching the stairs from the opposite direction, and we went down together. Morgan Rees was in the hall, a bulky envelope in his hand.

"Clare," – he came to meet me – "I'm so sorry, but I shan't be able to make our walk after all. I've been waiting all week

43

for these notes to arrive, and I really must work on them. In fact, I've had an early breakfast in order to get down to it straight away. Will you forgive me?"

"Don't worry, I'll explore by myself. I don't envy you, having to work on a morning like this."

I followed the Dacombes into the dining-room. Dick Harvey's table was empty, a marmalade-smeared plate evidence of his impatience to return to his find. The Misses Jones, with a bowl of porridge apiece, nodded and smiled, and across the room the Americans were busy with their orange juice and soft-boiled eggs.

I sipped the hot coffee, my eyes following the school-teachers to their table. In spite of their reference to Aladdin, I couldn't imagine them as a joint Sinbad, creeping round at midnight pushing envelopes under doors. For that matter, none of the guests seemed in the least sinister.

It was a pity about Morgan's work; I'd have welcomed his company this morning. Nevertheless, I'd no intention of staying in the hotel, rushing to the window every time a car drew up. A little fresh air and exercise would do me good, and the breeze today alleviated yesterday's oppressive heat.

When I came out of the dining-room, the Mortimer children were in the hall, a boy and girl, aged about ten and seven. They were nice-looking children, tall for their ages, with thick dark hair like their father. To my surprise, the little girl approached me with a smile.

"Would you like to play ball?" she inquired hopefully.

"Well, I—"

"Just for a few minutes? We're going to the beach soon."

"All right," I said, "just for a few minutes." It couldn't be much fun for them here, I reflected, with no other children to play with.

We walked round the side of the house to the lawn under my window where I'd seen them earlier. I was informed that their names were Stuart and Emma, that I'd guessed their ages correctly, and that they lived in Surrey.

44

At Stuart's suggestion we played a version of Pig-in-the-Middle, which, since the 'pig' was invariably Emma, didn't seem too fair to me. After about ten minutes, Clive strolled round the corner.

"You've monopolised Clare quite long enough," he told his offspring. "Off you go now, and get ready for the beach."

"Thanks for playing with us!" Emma called over her shoulder as she ran after her brother.

"Lovely kids," I said, watching them go.

"Of course – they take after their father!"

"Yes, I noticed that."

I'd meant their physical likeness, but as soon as I'd spoken, realised that my comment could have – indeed, from his pleased expression, had – been taken as a personal compliment.

"What are you going to do with yourself today?" he asked as we walked slowly back towards the entrance.

"I thought I'd walk up the hill there and see what's on the other side."

He grinned. "Because it's there?"

"Something like that."

"All by yourself?"

"Yes, unfortunately, but I'll take a book with me."

As we went inside, Pauline and the children were coming down the stairs, armed with rugs, buckets and spades. I nodded goodbye to them and went up to my room to prepare for my own outing.

Ten minutes later I set off, planning, as I'd told Clive, to follow the path beyond the hotel and aim for the little pine wood I'd seen from my window.

The path itself petered out almost at once into a pebbly sheep track, climbing quite steeply up the rough grassy slope. The bracken, knee-high and already tipped with gold, brushed my bare legs with a feathery caress. A rabbit scuttled from almost under my feet.

45

After climbing steadily for a while, I turned to look back the way I'd come. Even from this height, the view was breathtaking. Below me and slightly to my left, the Carreg Coed lay sprawling between its gravelled car park and its neat gardens. The Dacombes, I saw, were back on the tennis court; I could just recognise their tiny figures.

Beyond the hotel, hidden in places as it dipped to follow the lie of the land, the white road along which I had come yesterday ribboned its way through the valley. On its far side, a patchwork of fields, separated from each other by low stone walls, lay in a motley of gold and green, stretching away to a cluster of buildings on the horizon, which must be the nearest village.

My view to the right was obscured by a jutting of the hillside, but the road fell away in the direction of the Plas Dinas, fringed on this side by tall, spare pine trees, dark green in the mellow sunshine.

I drew a deep breath of mountain air, and resumed my climb. The next time I turned, the view was cut off by a bluff of rock – I was in a little dip on the fringe of the pine wood. When I came out above it, I should be able to see round the projection right down to the foot of the valley.

Behind me in the stillness, a twig cracked suddenly. I turned, my heart accelerating. There was no one in sight. Ahead of me, a bird flapped up out of the grass, squawking shrilly. Something had alarmed it – and I hadn't moved.

Deliberately I relaxed my clenched hands. I was on a Welsh hillside, for goodness' sake, not in some notorious no-go area. Nevertheless, danger stalked even remote woodlands these days – and perhaps, considering the night's events, these woodlands more than most. Belatedly, it occurred to me that it had hardly been wise to come out alone.

Another twig cracked, and my control snapped with it. I turned swiftly from the shadows of the wood and started back up the slope as my imagination pelted me with possibilities:

46

they'd discovered I wasn't Goldilocks – Aladdin had arrived and somehow knew where I was . . .

The figure of a man loomed suddenly on the edge of my vision. I screamed and stumbled, and a hand snaked out and caught me as Clive Mortimer's voice exclaimed breathlessly,

"Hey, hang on – I didn't mean to scare you."

I shook his hand off and stood panting, still poised for flight. Was this Sinbad?

He said, "I say, I did give you a jolt, didn't I? I'm awfully sorry."

The breath was still a hard knot in my throat. "Were you following me?" I demanded unevenly.

He shrugged smilingly. "You hinted back at the hotel that you'd welcome some company."

I should have to watch my words more carefully; following the supposed compliment, he must have taken my unthinking remark as an invitation.

"I thought you were going to the beach?"

"Not I, ma'am. Pauline's taken the kids with a packed lunch; it's not worth going that far unless you make a day of it, and as I've a golf date with the Zimmermans at two, I had to opt out."

My breath was steadying now. "I see."

"Are you making for anywhere in particular?"

I hesitated. I wasn't afraid any more, but nor did I want the company of Clive Mortimer and his dark, assessing eyes; though I could hardly say so.

"I was aiming for that crop of rocks; there should be a wonderful view from there."

"May I join you?"

The question was perfunctory, since he was already walking beside me. Together we went back down the slope to the pine wood.

"You said last night you weren't interested in climbing or golf," Clive commented. "It seems a odd place to find a girl like you all alone."

I thought of Aladdin and my determination to play along with him. If, as Jack said, we were to pretend to be lovers, it would be wise to establish that now. Also, whether or not Clive really was Sinbad, it might help to keep him at arm's length.

So I said lightly, "I'm not really alone − or at least, not for long. My friend should have come with me, but he was delayed. He'll be here in time for lunch."

Intent on my lines, I hadn't noticed the little trickle of water running under the trees and my feet slithered suddenly on a pile of wet leaves. Clive's hand, warm on my wind-cooled arm, steadied me.

"Are you an item, then, you and this chap?"

I looked back at him with raised eyebrows and he gave an embarrassed laugh. "None of my business, eh? You're right, of course. Well, he's a lucky bloke. I hope he realises it."

We were through the wood now and the wind, which had been sifting through the pinetops above us, met us head-on, making me gasp.

We scrambled up the rough ground, his hand under my elbow. The grey, flat-topped rock stretched like a natural platform, affording a magnificent outlook. Falling away from our feet went the rocky scree, dwindling farther down to isolated boulders and outcrops until it levelled out on the easier slopes with a covering of grass. In the distance, the valley road lay white and dusty, with a minute beetle-car crawling along it. Could that be Aladdin?

I tore my eyes away, scanning instead the far hillside where a quarry was eating away at its side like a wasting disease. And away to our right lay the indented coastline and the sea. Braced against the wind, my hair streaming behind me, I was filled with exhilaration at the beauty of it all.

"You look like some spirit of the hills," Clive said unexpectedly. "You'd better come down, in case a sudden gust blows you off."

My gaze returned to the steep rocks falling vertically from where I stood, and I took an involuntary step backwards. Clive had seated himself behind the shelter of some bushes, from where he could still see across the valley. Since it seemed churlish not to, I sat down beside him.

He fished in his pocket for cigarettes. "Do you smoke?"

I shook my head.

"Mind if I do?"

"No."

He lit a cigarette, inhaled deeply, then leant his head back and blew smoke circles at the sky.

"Tell me about yourself," he invited.

Dangerous ground; suppose he knew the background of the real Goldilocks, and this was some kind of test?

"Nothing very interesting," I hedged, realising with dismay just how careful I would have to be.

"A mystery woman! That makes you even more exciting!" He reached for my hand, but I sat forward, managing to evade it without giving the impression of doing so.

"What about you?" I countered. "How long have you been married?"

"Not very subtle, lovely Clare! But since you ask, the answer is ten years. Which doesn't automatically blind me to other women's attractions. However," he continued when I didn't speak, "I have the feeling that won't cut much ice with you. Right?"

"Right."

"Oh well, win some, lose some. You can't blame me for trying."

Curiously, the wariness between us fell away and we both relaxed. It was as though his macho self-image forced him to try his luck, but having failed, he bore me no ill-will. Further, he proved, surprisingly, to be an interesting and informative companion, naming the various hills and bays that lay spread before us.

By now completely at ease with him, I'd have welcomed his company at the hotel during the wait for Aladdin, but he was lunching at the golf club with the Zimmermans.

I glanced at my watch. It was already after eleven-thirty, and some of the anxiety of the previous night returned, producing a leaden feeling inside me.

Clive had seen my movement, and consulted his own watch. "Yes, it's time we were getting back. Mustn't keep the boyfriend waiting!"

He took my hand and this time I made no attempt to withdraw it. It was oddly comforting. Side by side, we went back down the slippery hillside to the Carreg Coed and parted at the gateway. Since Pauline had taken the car, he was intending to catch the hourly bus along the main road. I stood looking after him and he turned at the corner, raising his hand in a wave. Then he was gone.

With a tightening of my stomach muscles, I turned and walked into the hotel.

The hall was deserted, and a faint smell of cooking came from the kitchen. Through the glass wall I could see the old ladies placidly knitting in the lounge. I started up the stairs, realised I hadn't collected my key, and went back down again. It was twelve-fifteen. Had he arrived?

Reaching for the key, I wished passionately that I'd never come to this wretched place, and was safely at home in my cheerless, impersonal flat. My moment of panic on the hill had shown how flimsy was my attempt at bravado. How could I have imagined for one moment that I could beat these people at their own game? I must have been insane! I should have left after breakfast, as I'd first intended, and been miles away by this time. Now, it was too late. I would have to go through with it.

As I was turning away, my eyes lit on the postcard rack on the desk. I picked out three at random, dropped some coins into the box provided for the purpose, and went back up the stairs.

The door of the room next to mine stood open, awaiting the arrival of its new occupant. So he wasn't here yet. I glanced inside as I passed, and came to a sudden halt as I caught sight of a piece of paper propped up on the dressing-table.

Another note from Sinbad? Without conscious thought I darted into the room, snatched it up and crammed it into my pocket. Then I was outside and fumbling at my own door.

I closed it firmly and leant against it, breathing deeply as I withdrew the crumpled paper and smoothed it out with trembling fingers.

Not from Sinbad, anyway. It was typed on hotel stationery and read: *Miss Lawrence unavoidably detained after slight road accident, but hopes to arrive tomorrow.* It was signed *G Davies.*

I released my breath in a long sigh. The fates were with me. If Aladdin had read that, he wouldn't have established contact with me, and Sinbad would have wondered why.

Once more I climbed on the dressing-stool and stowed my latest trophy away with the others. It was unlikely Mrs Davies would refer to it, she'd naturally assume he'd received it. I wiped wet palms down my shorts. Now, all I could do was try to fill in the time until he arrived.

I washed, changed into a dress, and sat down on the window-seat to write my postcards.

I addressed the first one to Matthew, explaining my inadvertent change of itinerary. (If only I'd gone to Somerset!) Then, trying to think of something bland to say, I wrote another to a girl at work.

I'd just finished the second card when there was a tap on the door. My head snapped up.

"Yes?"

"It's Morgan, Clare. I was wondering if you'd join me for a drink before lunch?"

"Oh Morgan, I'd love to!" A wave of grateful relief washed over me; I shouldn't after all have to sit waiting by myself.

"Did you enjoy your walk?" he asked, as we went together down the stairs.

"Yes, thanks. I went up the hill."

51

"Perhaps we could go farther afield this afternoon? I've done quite enough work for a Saturday!"

"Oh, I—" For the second time I embarked on the story I'd been given. "I'm expecting someone any minute. I'm – not sure I'll be free this afternoon."

I realised with a sudden sinking of the heart that Aladdin would expect me to spend all my time with him, as would be only natural for lovers. But how could I be constantly with him, without giving myself away?

Morgan glanced at my face, took my arm and led me into the cocktail lounge.

"A girlfriend?" he asked. It was differently phrased from Clive's question, but it meant the same.

I looked away. "No."

"Oh, well, the luck of the draw, I suppose. I might have known you were too pretty to be unattached."

The cocktail lounge was small and bright, the large semi-circular bar unit taking up most of the room. There were a few tables round the wall.

"Don't let's sit in the window," I said quickly.

He raised his eyebrows but made no comment. We threaded our way past some people I hadn't seen before – passing trade, no doubt – to a table at the far side.

"Now, what's it to be? Sherry?"

"Could I have a gin and tonic?"

"In need of something stronger? Of course."

I looked at him sharply, but he'd turned away to order. The clock above the bar moved jerkily forward one minute. The hands pointed to twelve thirty-five. My heart was beginning to pound again. I wished I dared confide in Morgan, but how did I know I could trust him? The situation was too potentially dangerous to rely on feminine intuition.

"Here we are." He was beside me, setting the drinks on the table.

At least he'd be with me, to help me over the initial meeting. Then a thought struck me, jerking my hand so that the drink spilled on the table. I'd be expected to introduce him to Aladdin!

Panic engulfed me. Why hadn't I thought of this? Why in the name of heaven hadn't I tried to find out the real name of the man due any minute? Was there time to run out and ask Mrs Davies? Yet what possible reason could I give?

But before I could formulate any emergency plan, the sound of a car turning off the road reached us through the open window and the next minute a dark car swept past. It was too late.

There was the scrunch of feet on the gravel, but the entrance lay between us and the car park and the new arrival didn't pass the window. I imagined rather than heard the whisper of the swing doors, and voices in the hall. He'd probably look for me in the lounge. Would he take his case upstairs? Had I any chance of a hasty look at the register? How many seconds had I?

A ruddy-faced man at the next table laughed uproariously. *Oh, be quiet*, I implored him silently. *How can I hear—?*

Then suddenly the man who must surely be Aladdin was in the doorway. My hands clenched in an uncontrollable spasm and I felt myself go rigid. His eyes moved swiftly down the room, found mine, and he stiffened. There was on his face a frozen look of disbelief. Oh God! I thought raspingly, oh God!

For a timeless aeon which could only have been seconds, we stared across the room at each other. Then, with an obvious effort, he forced the semblance of a smile and made his way over to me, his eyes still locked on mine. He bent down, kissed me lightly, and said, with only a slight tremor in his voice, "Hello, darling. Sorry I got held up."

I tried to speak, but no sound came. Carefully I unflexed my knotted fingers and tried again.

"Hello, Philip," I said.

Chapter Six

'"I can't explain myself, I'm afraid sir," said Alice,
"because I'm not myself, you see."
"I don't see," said the Caterpillar.'
Lewis Carroll: *Alice in Wonderland*

MORGAN cleared his throat. "Can I get you a drink?"

With an enormous effort, I pulled myself together. "I'm so sorry. Morgan, this is Philip Hardy. Philip – Morgan Rees."

The two men shook hands and Morgan excused himself and went over to the bar. I didn't dare look at Philip, but I could feel him staring at me. I thought wildly – but it can't be him! Was there some mistake? Had Philip arrived by chance, and was Aladdin still to come?

Perhaps I was wrong and the plot, whatever it was, was perfectly innocent? Philip couldn't be involved in anything shady.

Or could he? I'd already been disillusioned on that score, three months ago. I'd convinced myself it had been a temporary slip, but had it in fact been only the beginning? When Philip flung himself out of Matthew's firm, had it been into really deep waters?

"Gin and bitters." Morgan put the glass in front of Philip. "A topper, Clare?"

I shook my head, needing all my wits about me now.

"Have you come far?" Morgan inquired pleasantly.

"Only from Bristol, this morning. I couldn't get away as

54

early as I'd hoped, so decided to break the journey. I suppose you arrived yesterday, Clare?"

"Yes." I wondered if Morgan noticed how jerky our voices were.

"Did you have a reasonable journey?"

"It was all right."

Breaking a lengthening silence, Morgan said, "Clare tells me she's not interested in fishing or golf. How about you?"

Philip turned to look at him. "What? Oh – I do fish a little, yes."

Out in the hall the lunch gong sounded. As we rose to our feet, Philip's hand on my arm was like a vice. "Have you arranged for me to sit at your table?"

"Er – no, I – didn't think."

We reached the dining-room, where Morgan left us with a cheerful "See you!" to go to his own table. Harry the waiter turned from the serving hatch and I saw the leap of interest in his eyes.

Philip said crisply, "Would you lay a place for me at Miss Laurie's table, please."

Harry glanced at me with a look of triumph. "Of course, sir."

I seated myself in my usual place and Philip sat down beside me. Harry, who had started to lay the second place opposite mine, moved the cutlery accordingly.

The minute he left us, Philip said in a low, vicious voice, "What the hell do you think you're playing at, Clare?"

It was like a slap in the face – yet what could I expect? He'd had as much of a shock as I, and it had obviously been no more pleasant. He was not likely to address me in the gentle, bantering way I'd been used to.

I hoped my own voice was steady. "The same game as you, of course."

"I don't believe it!"

But he must! "I have some information for you," I said, and at last looked up and met his eyes. They were hard and cold, and I saw that his face was thinner than when we'd last met. He looked older. His mouth, which had always had a smile for me, was tight-lipped and drawn, almost cruel. I could expect no quarter from this new Philip – I had to convince him I was all I pretended to be.

"My God!" he said tonelessly. "It was a bit – unnecessary – sending you, wasn't it?"

"I'm your cover," I said calmly, marvelling at myself.

He made an impatient gesture. "Look, as soon as this meal's over, we're going where there's no danger of eavesdroppers and I intend to get to the bottom of this. In the meantime, perhaps you'd make an effort to appear glad to see me. You're acting as if I'd murdered your grandmother."

Harry came back with two bowls of soup, and it was a marvel to me that I could swallow it. In the space of ten minutes, everything had been shaken up like a kaleidoscope and fallen back into an entirely different pattern. Philip was Aladdin – Aladdin was Philip – and even if I wanted to, there was nowhere I could run where Philip would not find me.

Roast Welsh lamb followed, with rich gravy and mint sauce, but my throat was closed and I managed only a mouthful or two before laying down my knife and fork. Philip was doing no better, and with a sudden movement pushed his plate away.

"It's no good, I can't eat and nor, it seems, can you. Once we've sorted ourselves out, perhaps we can act more convincingly."

He stood up, and as Harry anxiously approached, said curtly, "We won't bother with the dessert, thank you." His hand on my elbow, he guided me out of the room.

"Wait here while I take my case up."

It was an order, but I'd had no intention of following him and went instead to the ladies' room. He was right, I looked as woebegone and frightened as I felt, my face pale beneath the tan. Any more shocks like this, and I'd have to revert to full make-up after all. I freshened my lipstick, pinched my cheeks to give them more colour, and

56

went back into the hall as Philip was coming down the stairs.

He stood aside for me to go through the swing doors, took my arm and led the way to his car. He didn't release me until he had opened the door and helped me in. I wondered dully whether it was force of habit or if he thought I might make a run for it. Yet he couldn't know how frightened I was.

He got in beside me, and the grotesqueness of the situation struck me afresh as I recalled all the times we'd set off together in this car, often with Matthew in the back.

But Matthew was the last person I wanted to think about just now. If he found out – I wrenched my thoughts away from him.

Philip meanwhile had turned left on the main road and set off along a stretch new, presumably, to both of us. He drove, as always, competently and fast. I watched his long, slim hands firm on the wheel, still trying to adjust to his being Aladdin. It was unbelievable that I could actually feel frightened of Philip, who'd always been so eager to please me. But I didn't need to remind myself that this wasn't the same man; this was a side of him that I, and, I prayed, my uncle, had never seen before.

And all the time I was trying to think what I could say to him. It would need to be more detailed than if Aladdin had been the expected stranger. Philip would be in an inquisitorial mood and I could not allow myself even one mistake. My mouth was taut and dry, and I could almost taste the nervous pumping of my heart.

Neither of us spoke, and I wondered what thoughts were going round his head. After a while he turned the car off the smooth surface and we jolted over the rough ground and came to rest overlooking a small natural lake. It was a lovely scene, with drooping willows and long-tailed water birds, but neither of us gave it more than a perfunctory glance. Philip switched off the engine, wound down his window, and turned to face me.

"Well?"

I clung to what I knew. "You want to discuss the plan?"

He brushed that aside. "What I *want* is to know how in God's name you got mixed up in all this. I still can't believe we're having this conversation."

"Nor can I," I admitted feelingly.

He frowned. "Weren't you expecting me?"

A warning light flashed in my head. That had been a slip, and I was still floundering for an answer when he said suddenly, "Doesn't Bryn know about us?"

Bryn – Jack? "I didn't tell him," I said truthfully.

"But you knew I was Aladdin?"

"No."

"That figures – or you'd never have agreed to come. Bryn and his bloody secrecy!" He gave a harsh laugh. "Poor Clare, no wonder you looked a bit white around the gills!"

"And you didn't know I was Goldilocks?"

That should convince him. It seemed to; he looked at me sharply, then away again. "Of course not – I'd no idea you were involved. I was expecting the Lawrence girl, though actually Bryn just said he was sending 'one of his birds'. I presume the description fits?"

His tone was an insult, but before I could think of a reply he burst out, "God, Clare, where did you meet him? And when? I know he's attractive to women and there's always a crowd of them around him, but you! I'd never have thought—" He broke off and ran a hand through his hair.

"You mean," I said, asserting myself at last, "that he's rather different from you?"

There was a pause. Then he said quietly, "I suppose I deserved that. Tell me one thing: did you know him while we were engaged?"

"Yes," I lied.

"I thought there must be someone. Where did you meet?"

I hesitated.

"At one of the galleries?"

"Yes," I acknowledged, grateful for the let-out.

58

We sat in silence for a few minutes, each digesting the information we had gleaned. It seemed almost certain that Bryn was Jack, and in charge of the operation. Was he intending to join us, or busy establishing alibis in London? I couldn't ask – I was supposed to know the answer.

As to his reputation with women and my own part in it, I was powerless to defend myself, though the scorn in Philip's voice still rankled.

"He must be pretty sure of you," he said after a while, "to entrust you with this. But I suppose if he didn't know we knew each other—"

"What difference does that make?"

I felt him tense, and waited nervously for another of those uncharacteristic outbursts. But he merely said tightly, "You're right, none at all, though you must admit it's one hell of a coincidence. Come to think of it, since you're so heavily involved, what price that sanctimonious little scene at Conningley? Believe me, it would upset Matthew far more to learn of your defection than it did of mine."

I bent my head.

"Or is your affection for him just a blind?"

"No!" I said sharply.

"Then I can't pretend to understand."

Nor I, though I couldn't say so.

"You didn't know at the time, did you?" Philip went on.

"At the time?"

"Of the fire."

"Oh. No." I paused, and added for more emphasis, "No, I didn't."

"Nor did I. For what it's worth, that's the truth. But since it's all gone through now, I'm damned if I see why we shouldn't share in the profit. Agreed?"

"Definitely," I said whitely.

"Well, you might as well tell me where they are, then."

I frowned. "Don't you know?"

"Only the final part – so many paces after such and such.

But in true Bryn fashion, I haven't been told where those paces have to be taken."

"At Cefn Fawr Castle."

"And where the devil's that?"

I shook my head. He reached over to the back seat for a map. I didn't make any attempt to look at it.

"Seems to be on the coast, about fifteen miles away. Presumably we're supposed to reconnoitre?"

"Yes, either today or tomorrow. Beanstalk is scheduled for Tuesday."

He looked at me through narrowed eyes. "Quite the little confidante, aren't you? Have you got a plan of the place?"

Damn! I'd intended to bring it, but the shock of seeing him had driven such practical considerations out of my head.

"Not with me, I'm afraid."

"What do you mean, not with you?" His voice sharpened. "Good God, you didn't leave it in your room?"

"It's hidden, don't worry."

"Under the mattress, I suppose." His voice was heavy with sarcasm.

"I'm not a complete fool, Philip."

There was a short silence, then he said brusquely, "I'm sorry, I can't seem to adjust to your being well-schooled in all this."

Hardly surprising.

He gave a sigh of exasperation. "Well, if we haven't got the plan we can't go now, which is a bit of a bind."

"We don't really need it," I urged, cursing my stupidity and conscious of 'the Lawrence girl's' imminent arrival. "The corridor won't be hard to locate."

But he shook his head decidedly. "No, we'll leave it till tomorrow – I'm not in the mood for treasure-hunting. Anything else to report?"

"Only that the shipment has been arranged," I said, parrot-wise.

"Uh-huh. And the Zimmermans? I didn't see them at lunch."

That really shook me. I said feebly, "They were lunching at the golf club. Clive was meeting them there at twelve-thirty."

"Clive?"

"Just someone at the hotel. I met him out on the hill this morning."

"Sinbad?"

My eyes flew to his. "I don't know – don't you?"

"No, only that he's here. Another example of Bryn not letting the right hand know what the left's doing."

His voice was bitter. He was staring straight ahead of him, across the silver waters of the little lake. This new Philip, tight-lipped and aloof, took a bit of getting used to. After all the years of his striving to please me, it was disconcerting to discover that I quite obviously meant nothing to him. I was strictly on my own, and heaven help me if I put a foot wrong.

He turned his head, meeting my eyes. "So what do we do now?"

I looked away. "I don't know. There's not much point in going back yet. Perhaps we could drive to the nearest beach? It would pass the time."

"I thought you loathed beaches?"

"It was only a suggestion. Have you a better one?"

"No, my brain's not functioning this afternoon. But as you say, since we're supposed to be in love – though God knows why it was necessary to have that embellishment – it would hardly be in keeping to sit reading newspapers in the lounge. Very well, the beach it is."

"Unless we try the castle, after all," I suggested again.

"I told you, I'm not up to it," Philip said baldly. "Just one thing more, before we start making sand pies: how's Matthew?"

I bit my lip. "He seems – all right."

"When did you see him last?"

"Just before I left. The day before yesterday."

He turned to me then, and I didn't like the expression in his eyes. "Well, I must say, you've more nerve than I have. At least I broke away before I got in too deep."

"You had no option," I said tartly, "you were thrown out."

"*Touché*. And you, so far, have been more circumspect?"

"Precisely." The brittle little voice didn't sound like mine. If only I knew what it was all about, how serious it was, if there was somebody I could warn, and who, if anyone, I could trust at the hotel!

"The Zimmermans," I began hesitantly as Philip bumped the car back on to the road.

"Don't worry – they won't give any sign of recognising me. They're pretty well briefed. I saw them in Chicago last month."

"So they – know all about it?"

He glanced at me with amused impatience. "They have the right, wouldn't you say, since they're the buyers?"

So we had something to sell. What was it that was hidden in the dark passage of Cefn Fawr? Drugs, diamonds, state secrets? Was Philip now a drug dealer or a foreign agent? The idea seemed too ludicrous for serious consideration, but that the stakes were high, I no longer doubted.

The sun suddenly ceased to warm me, and I shivered.

"Break in the weather ahead." Philip nodded in the direction of a large purple cloud which was draining the colour out of the sky like a giant sponge. "Looks as if we're in for a storm. It was forecast."

I gazed at the heavy cloud with foreboding. "Perhaps it will blow over."

"Not a chance, we're driving straight into it."

"Shall we turn round, then?"

He did not reply.

I sat with clenched hands, staring unseeingly through the windscreen at the berried hedgerows and golden fields lit by the stormy sunshine as the sky gradually darkened.

I had never felt so alone. The only person I could trust in my suddenly topsy-turvy world was three hundred miles away, and he was the one who at all costs must be spared knowledge of the affair.

The road began to wind tortuously downhill, and ahead of us lay the sea. We drove through a gateway into a car park, buying a ticket as we went, and Philip managed to find a place to park. The area was filled with station wagons, motor-bikes and cars, and on rising ground behind it I could see the clustered shapes of a caravan site.

I stepped out of the car, smoothing down my dress, and the strong wind blowing off the sea raised the gooseflesh on my arms. Particles of sand driven before it stung my bare legs like myriads of tiny darts. I was already sorry I'd suggested the beach, but I was allowed no second thoughts.

"Come on." Philip set off purposefully for the dunes and I meekly followed. The soft sand was heavy going and my shoes soon filled with it, cramping my toes. I stopped to take them off and hurried after him, the tired muscles pulling at the back of my knees.

He was waiting on the top of a sand-dune and as I joined him, the breath was knocked out of my body by the strength of the wind that hit me. My thin dress whipped stingingly round my legs.

"Healthy stuff," Philip commented. His open sandals were no hindrance, I thought resentfully, wiping the back of my hand across my mouth to remove the blowing sand. The wind licked through my dress, cold on my sun-warmed body, and I shivered again.

"Soon get warm!" said my companion briskly, and set off down the other side of the dune towards the sea. It was a long way out, and seemingly miles of hard brown sand, painfully ribbed, lay between it and us.

Philip strode without a second glance past sand castles, racing dogs, families playing cricket, children throwing balls and crab-filled pools. I almost ran to keep up with him, my body bent into the wind. I sensed that he welcomed the strong breeze, hoping it might clear his head of all the conflicting thoughts he must still have about me, and I knew nothing would have pleased him more than to walk away from me completely.

At last he stopped and turned with the semblance of a smile. "It might be quicker to drive round to Devon and catch the tide there." His eyes narrowed. "You're not cold, are you?"

"Of course I'm cold!" I snapped. "I've hardly any clothes on and the wind is bitter."

"Nonsense, a little fresh, nothing more." He surveyed me for a moment, then pulled off his camel sweater. "Put this on; it will be a pretty pass if you have to spend Tuesday in bed with a chill."

Which, of course, was his only concern. I pulled it fiercely over my head. It was deliciously comforting, warm from his body, and reaching down as far as the hem of my skirt. Philip stood watching as I doubled the cuffs over.

"You look about twelve," he said. "I just can't—"

His mouth hardened and he turned away.

"Can we go back now?" I asked meekly.

"Tired of it already? This was your idea, remember."

As he spoke, a large drop of rain the size of a penny fell on to the back of my hand. We both looked up. The purple cloud had spread alarmingly over the sky and now covered it completely.

"Come on!" He seized my hand and we started to run, the wind now helping us along, back towards the distant shelter of a café.

The rain began in earnest. All around us, people were hastily gathering together children, dogs and belongings, and starting to stream off the beach in straggling, disorganised groups. Almost directly overhead came a deafening crash. My nails dug into Philip's hand.

"Still afraid of thunder, Clare?" He'd teased me about that since childhood. "I've already been thunderstruck once today," he added with grim humour. "It won't strike twice in the same place."

At last we had reached the little café and pressed our way inside. It was already filled to capacity, but people were still pushing from behind. Another crash sounded, rolling round the hills behind us, and one or two children began to cry. Instinctively I edged closer to Philip, but he gave me a little push and said briskly, "Pull yourself together, there are worse things than thunder. If I can get to the counter I'll bring you a hot drink."

There were no free tables, but I moved against a window and, huddled into Philip's sweater, stood looking out at the desolate and deserted beach. It was not an inspiring sight, and I turned back to watch his progress in the queue. He was head and shoulders above the other holidaymakers, his blue shirt wet across the back, his face flushed from the rain and our race against it. With the colour in his cheeks, he looked all at once more like the Philip I remembered. But he wasn't, I reminded myself, and wondered whether, if I'd stuck by him when he left the company, he might not have become involved in all this.

He shouldered his way back to me with a steaming mug of tea. "God," he said, "what a place!"

The room was suddenly lit by a jag of lightning and another deafening peal broke overhead. The lights went out, but even as everyone exclaimed, came flickeringly on again. The tea in my mug sloshed over the rim.

"That was close!" someone said.

Philip looked down at me. "If you weren't hooked on danger you wouldn't be here, so why complain about the sound effects? At least we're not marooned in the castle."

I swallowed the scalding liquid, welcoming the pain as it seared my throat. The crowd, wet and restless, pressed against us, and all at once I was enveloped by nightmare. The hot, damp atmosphere, the noise, the flushed faces all around me, had an quality about them that was suddenly frightening. The only reality was Philip, whom I'd known most of my life, and he was watching me with the cold, indifferent eyes of a stranger.

I tried to draw a breath to steady myself, couldn't, and immediately panicked.

"Philip, I've got to get out of here!"

"My dear girl, look at the weather!"

"I can't – breathe!" My voice rose.

He took the cup out of my hand and placed it with his own on the nearest table. Then he gripped my hand and elbowed a way through the crowd. In a moment he had the door open and we were met by the wild wet wind. I leant on the little wooden rail that ran round the verandah, gulping in lungfuls of the strong air.

"I'm sorry," I said, when I was able to speak. "That's never happened before, but I didn't sleep well last night, and then today has been somewhat – stressful—" My voice tailed off.

Philip ignored my apology, staring across the rainswept wastes. "I must say you choose your rare days at the seaside with discernment. Better now?"

"Yes thank you. Let's go back to the car."

"I'm not driving anywhere in this deluge."

"At least we'll be out of the rain. I can't go back inside, and I'm getting soaked. So are you."

He turned, leaning against the rail as the wind tore at his hair. "I can't help feeling," he said sardonically, "that as an accomplice, you're something of a liability."

"What was that about getting a chill before Tuesday?"

He straightened. "Yes, indeed. Bryn would never forgive me."

Without waiting for him, I stumbled down the steps and round the corner in the direction of the car park. In two minutes I was drenched to the skin, my feet squelching uncomfortably in my shoes. Philip caught up with me, took my arm, and led me, head bent, to the car. As we settled ourselves, the windows steamed up with the dampness of our clothes, enclosing us in unwanted privacy. I took a handkerchief out of my bag and rubbed ineffectually at my face and hands.

"I'll put the heater on," Philip said. "You'll soon dry off.

How about a round of *Men of Harlech* to keep our spirits up?
Has Bryn taught you the Welsh version?"

I turned my face away from him.

"Or have you better things to do together than learning
Welsh?"

I spun round. "*Stop* it, Philip!"

He glanced at me with raised eyebrows, and I went on more
calmly, "It's not my fault we're compelled to work together;
it's no easier for me, you know, and your snide innuendoes
don't help. Is it revenge because we split up?"

I thought he wasn't going to reply. Then he said quietly,
"No, Clare, it's not that. I'd known it was coming for some
time, and even if I hadn't, I couldn't have blamed you in the
circumstances. You'd have had to love me a great deal to have
stood by me then, and I never fooled myself on that score."

I laced my fingers together, keeping my eyes on them. "Then
what—?"

"I suppose I'd a pretty idealised picture of you. So when
I saw you in the bar, and realised that not only were you
Goldilocks, and therefore up to your neck in this unsavoury
business, but also that you were one of the girls Bryn boasts
about so openly—"

He broke off and I sat in helpless silence until he went
on, "So I'm afraid you'll have to excuse my behaviour – I'm
still shell-shocked. It's not every day you discover a girl you
thought you knew, and had loved for some time, is just a cheap
little crook."

Pride came to my rescue. "Coming from you," I said icily,
"that is rich."

"It is, isn't it? And they say women are illogical."

The sheets of water still fell relentlessly. And it had been
such a lovely morning, on the hillside with Clive. Quite suddenly, I couldn't take any more; I needed to get away from him,
back to the privacy of my bedroom, where I could take stock of
this new situation. When I'd left it, I'd been preparing to meet
Aladdin – and I'd thought things were complicated then.

67

"Well," I said, keeping my voice light, "if you've finished insulting me, perhaps you'll take me back to the hotel."

"Visibility's not more than a few yards. We could run off a precipice."

"Would it matter?"

I felt him look at me. There was a pause, then he said, "Clare, I'm sorry." His voice had gone flat. "Really. I'm being most unprofessional about this; I'd no right to speak to you as I did. As you say, if we have to work together, it's pointless to erect this barrier of hostility."

He paused, but I didn't speak.

"Will you accept my apology?"

"For business reasons?" I asked bitterly.

"No, because I see I hurt you. Yes, I know I meant to, but now I'm sorry."

"Forget it."

We drove back to the hotel in complete silence, Philip bending forward to peer through the wall of rain, I leaning back in my seat with my eyes closed and my tangled hair slowly drying round my face. The thunder and the sleepless night, combined with the emotional upheaval of the last few hours, had given me a raging headache.

It was still raining. Philip dropped me at the front door and drove on to park the car. The hands of the grandfather clock pointed to five-thirty – almost exactly the time I'd arrived yesterday, with Gareth's fateful note in my handbag.

I went up to my room without seeing anyone and took a couple of pills for my headache. Then, slipping out of my damp clothes, I lay thankfully down on the bed. As I closed my eyes, I heard Philip's door open and close. Almost immediately, I slept.

Chapter Seven

'Riddles of death . . .'

Shelley: *Hellas*

THE SOUND of footsteps pounding past my door and children's voices calling awoke me: the young Mortimers, returning from their visit to the beach. I hoped bleakly they had enjoyed it more than I had mine. I turned my head to look at the clock. Just time for a quick bath before dinner.

As I fastened the zip of my dress, the gong sounded. I reached automatically for the scent bottle then hesitated, remembering it had been Philip's birthday present. Telling myself not to be stupid, I applied some, and, with a final check in the mirror, opened the door.

From the hall came the clamour of voices as people made their way to the dining-room. Philip was awaiting me at the foot of the stairs. Now for the public affection decreed by Bryn.

"Hello!" I said brightly. "I only just made it – I was asleep twenty minutes ago!"

It was amazing how natural I sounded.

Philip said easily, "Good for you; it will have done you a power of good."

Top marks to him, too, though I guessed it was whisky, not sleep, which had helped him relax. He took my arm and we went together into the dining-room. The Zimmermans were already at their table, and I caught their fractional immobility as Philip and I entered.

Morgan, who had been standing talking to the old ladies, turned as we approached and forestalled Philip in pulling out my chair.

"If I'm not speaking out of turn, you're looking very lovely this evening." I smiled at him, and was surprised to see the seriousness of his expression.

"Is something wrong?" I asked quickly.

"I hope not; we're just a little concerned about Dick; there's been no sight nor sound of him since he left early this morning."

I said comfortably, "Well, he was late for dinner last night, too."

"Yes, but he was expecting an overseas call at six, from some friends holidaying in Greece. They're working together on some project, and he was looking forward to hearing how they'd got on."

"And did they phone?"

"Yes; not best pleased, according to Mrs Davies. I can't believe he'd have forgotten it." Morgan glanced at Philip, who was still standing. "Sorry – I'm intruding."

He was turning away, but I said swiftly, "You don't think he could have got into difficulties?" I'd liked the shy little man with his schoolboy enthusiasm.

"Oh, he's probably just got a flat tyre or something. On the other hand, this afternoon's storm wouldn't have been pleasant in the kind of places he goes to. There probably wasn't much shelter."

I'd been too overwhelmed by Philip's arrival to register Dick Harvey's absence at lunch-time. I glanced at his empty table and gave a little shiver.

"Is he a climber?" Philip inquired.

"No, an amateur archaeologist. As Clare says, he'll no doubt come breezing in late, as he did last night. But I'm keeping you from your dinner."

He went on to his own table and Harry approached and handed me the menu. I couldn't concentrate on it. At the next table, the old ladies were twittering like agitated sparrows. Over by the window, the honeymooners sat silently, close together. Even the loud-voiced Miss Norton was subdued this evening.

The sound of approaching footsteps turned every head in the room, but it was Clive and Pauline who entered. In an uneasy silence they walked to their table. Clive made some laughing comment to Elmer Zimmerman as he passed, but it elicited only a faint smile in response.

The general feeling of apprehension increased throughout the meal. People spoke seldom, and then in low voices. And all the time the rain rattled like tiny pellets against the glass and the wind blew gustily down the wide chimney.

It was certainly no time for Philip and me to engage in our prescribed flirting and we tacitly abandoned it, resorting to the same pattern of sporadic conversation as the rest of them.

"Did you and Uncle stay here once, a few years ago?" I asked suddenly.

He looked at me quickly, eyes narrowing. "What makes you ask that?"

"I remembered him talking about that holiday you had, and the name Dryffyd seemed familiar."

"No, it wasn't here, it was an hotel further down the road."

"The Plas Dinas?"

"That's right – where we were supposed to meet up yesterday."

Which confirmed my guess.

I returned to my dinner and after a moment, Philip, too, picked up his fork again.

There was a slight diversion towards the end of the meal, when Emma Mortimer appeared in her nightdress, complaining of a rattling window which was keeping her awake. Pauline shooed her out again, and went up with her to wedge it.

I laid my spoon on my plate, abandoning the last of the Peach Melba.

"Do they serve coffee?" Philip asked.

"Yes, in the lounge."

71

As we walked through the hall, the Mortimers and Morgan were standing chatting together.

"I hope you weren't wanting a brandy, Philip," Morgan said, indicating a notice pinned to the closed door of the cocktail lounge. It read: *Sorry, bar closed from 7–9 p.m.*

"Fortunately we're only in search of coffee," Philip answered, and as we went on into the lounge, they turned and followed us.

Several people were already there, and I seated myself in much the same place as I had the previous evening. This time, though, there was no Dick Harvey talking excitedly about his find. I glanced anxiously at my watch. Eight-thirty; surely even if he'd had a puncture, as Morgan had suggested, he'd have been back by now.

"Coffee, Miss – er – Laurie?" The fluttery Miss Bunting was beside me. Philip immediately stood up.

"Let me do that – you sit down."

"No, really, it's all right—"

"Please, I insist."

"Well, in that case—" She smiled uncertainly and seated herself beside me. Until now, I'd not spoken more than a couple of words to her, and as we embarked on a rather stilted conversation, I was able to study her more closely. She seemed nervous, talking in a quick, low voice and blinking rapidly as she did so, but this might be habitual. I reflected that if I spent much time in Miss Norton's company, I might well be nervous myself.

As though my thought had conjured the woman up, she loomed suddenly above me. "I see you've deserted me, Joan!" she announced with mock severity, and Miss Bunting fluttered even more.

Miss Norton held out a large hand and I obediently put mine into it. "We've not met formally, have we? Eunice Norton."

"Clare Laurie," I said, "and may I introduce Philip Hardy?"

"Here for the golf, Mr Hardy?" Miss Norton inquired, as she joined us on the sofa.

"I'm afraid I don't play."

"No time, eh? I know you men! What line of business are you in?"

I held my breath, and after the briefest pause Philip answered, "Insurance."

"Ah, the triumph of hope over experience, as Dr Johnson remarked in a different context. We teach at a girls' school in Cardiff, for our sins."

"What subjects?" I asked, since it seemed to be expected.

"Joan takes music and drama, and I English Literature."

"Tell Clare about your hobby, Miss Norton," Clive suggested from across the room. "I'm sure she'd be interested."

I turned to her inquiringly, and she gave a pleased smile. "Actually, I'm researching the history of fairy tales."

My heart gave a jerk, though whether because of the hobby itself or Clive's drawing my attention to it, I couldn't be sure.

"My principal aim is conservation, you see," Miss Norton was continuing. "As I'm sure you're aware, every country has its own collection, and while many of them are known world-wide, others are in danger of being lost. Andrew Lang did a magnificent job on them some forty years ago, but I've been able to unearth quite a few he missed."

She glanced at me almost coyly. "In fact, the first volume has already been published. I've a copy with me, if you're interested."

"More power to your elbow!" Clive said jovially. "Speaking on behalf of all parents, anything that would make a change from Snow White or Jack and the Beanstalk would be more than welcome!"

Perhaps I imagined the brief, splintered silence. Certainly I held my own breath. But Miss Norton was still looking at me hopefully, and I forced myself to say, "Thank you, I'd love to see it."

I glanced at Clive but he was smiling benignly, to all appearances quite unaware of any undercurrents. It was Pauline who changed the subject, and to one no more comfortable.

"I do wish Dick would come," she exclaimed anxiously.

"Something must have happened, for him to be as late as this."

"Well done, darling; we've been doing our best to keep off that subject."

"Well, I'm sorry, but I'm really worried."

There was another silence, unmistakable this time, and in the middle of it Philip stood up, took my empty cup from my hand and replaced it with his on the trolley.

"You were going to look out that book for me, Clare."

"Yes, of course." I was glad to leave this suddenly claustrophobic room. "I'll get it now."

As we went out into the hall, he said in a low voice, "What was all that about? Sinbad playing silly beggars?"

"I've no idea."

"In any other circumstances, it would have been quite amusing; it's hard to associate Miss Norton with frog princes and sleeping beauties.

"Anyway, to business. I'd like to have a look at that plan." He glanced at the empty reception desk. "And perhaps we should order a packed lunch for tomorrow."

The day of reconnaissance. "Yes, let's do it now, while we think of it."

Philip pressed the bell on the desk, but as he did so, the telephone rang in the office behind and we heard Mr Davies say, "Carreg Coed Hotel." Then his voice tautened. "Yes? What's the trouble?"

I clutched at Philip's arm.

"Yes, that's right," Davies was saying. There was a long pause, then he said expressionlessly, "Oh, my God!" And again, "Oh, God. Yes – yes, of course – I suppose you must. There's nothing I can do? Very well."

There was a click as the phone was replaced. Philip and I waited. Wynne Davies appeared in the doorway, his face white with shock.

"It's Mr Harvey," he said, his voice shaking. "He's been found at the foot of a cliff, over at Pen-y-Coed. He's dead."

74

I made some incoherent exclamation and Philip said quickly, "The man who was late? How terrible – what happened?"

"No one seems to know. I suppose he lost his footing – it's very dangerous there. That was the police; they found an envelope in his pocket, addressed to him here. They want to look through his things to find out who they should notify."

Philip registered my rigidity. "Clare? Are you all right?"

"Take her to the bar, Mr Hardy – I'll come and open it now. As luck would have it, Dai took the day off for his sister's wedding, and I'm having to stand in for him. Come to that, I could do with a drink myself."

We crossed the hall together and Wynne Davies pulled up the grill and poured brandy into three glasses. Philip put one into my hand and made me drink it. The fumes went up the back of my nose and I choked.

"That's it," said Wynne Davies mechanically, and swallowed his own. "He asked for an early breakfast," he continued, almost to himself. "Never dreamed that was the last time I'd see him." He pulled himself together with an effort. "Would you mind looking after the bar for me, sir? I shan't be long, but I must go and tell Gwynneth."

Shoulders bent, he went out of the room. Philip was looking at me curiously.

"Come on, Clare, snap out of it – you hardly knew the man. I know it's a shock, but accidents do happen."

"It wasn't an accident."

Philip's hand, reaching for his glass, stopped in mid-air.

"What did you say?"

"I said it wasn't an accident." I'd been unaware of the thought until I heard myself stating it, but I accepted it without question.

"What the hell are you talking about?"

I took another gulp from my glass. "He was late for dinner last night because he'd found something exciting which he thought was valuable. He said he'd have to contact the authorities." My voice dwindled away.

I had his full attention now. "*What* did he find?"

"I don't know. He wouldn't tell us any more till he'd been back for another look."

"Did he say where it was?"

I shook my head.

"Who knew about this?"

"We all did."

"Not very wise to shout it abroad, but he wasn't to know that."

"He was such a nice, harmless little man." My voice rocked.

Philip said slowly, "So you reckon he found more than was good for him?"

"Either that, or someone thought he had."

"Meaning Sinbad?"

I stared at him. In my distress, I'd forgotten our unknown associate. "I suppose so."

"You're quite sure you don't know who Sinbad is?"

"Quite. It could be any of the men here: Andrew Dacombe, Clive, Morgan – presumably not Mr Zimmerman?"

"No, definitely not."

"It could even be Mr Davies," I said reflectively, but Philip shook his head.

"Not unless he's a bloody good actor."

"Poor Dick; if he'd gone next week, there'd have been nothing to find and he'd have been all right. How dreadful, to think his life hung on five days."

"Aren't you rather jumping the gun? What he found might be something altogether different and nothing whatever to do with us."

"But you don't really believe that."

He sighed. "I suppose not."

"Well, whatever it was, his mistake was in talking about it. Because without even being sure what he'd stumbled on, someone couldn't afford to take the risk."

Philip was gazing thoughtfully into his glass. "Where were all the people you mentioned, this morning?"

76

I tried to think back. "Morgan had some work to do – probably in his room. I met Clive on the hill. Mr Zimmerman and his wife went to the golf club, though I don't know what time, but you say they're in the clear anyway. Andrew and Cindy were playing tennis when I left, but I don't know for how long. Still, I can't see her being mixed up in this."

Philip said on a questioning note, "Cindy? Cinderella?"

Briefly, my precarious world rocked again. Then I shook my head. "No, I'm sure that's coincidence."

"But have you considered that it could be a woman?"

I hadn't. I said incredulously, "Who killed Dick Harvey?"

"It could be, if she was working to Bryn's orders." He looked at me levelly. "It wasn't you, was it, Clare?"

The breath left my body as if I'd been winded.

He continued, "It wouldn't have taken much to push him over. Those cliffs at Pen-y-Coed are lethal, covered with slippery grass. Matthew and I went there one day. There are warning notices all over the place."

He added impatiently, "Oh, stop looking like that, for God's sake. I wasn't serious, but I want to bring home to you just what it is you're involved in. And for what it's worth, even if we knew who Sinbad was, there's nothing we could do about it. Whether you like it or not, if he did kill Harvey, it was to protect us as much as himself."

I closed my eyes on a wave of nausea. "But Dick wasn't a threat to anyone," I protested faintly.

"He would have been, if he'd unearthed the loot. Just think about it – the whole operation scuppered at the last minute because he happened to bumble along."

I looked at Philip with something approaching hatred, and his eyes dropped from mine. But before he could speak, Pauline came hurrying into the room, her eyes wide.

"Have you heard? Oh Clare, isn't it terrible? I *knew* something was wrong! That nice little man! He gave Stuart one of his old coins." Her eyes filled with tears.

Philip moved behind the bar. "What can I get you? Mr Davies

left me in charge and I expect a fair bit of medicinal alcohol will be called for tonight."

Clive and Morgan came in with the Zimmermans, whom I studied with covert suspicion. They looked so ordinary – he slightly rotund, balding, bespectacled; she with permed hair, small round eyes and a tightly corseted figure. Yet they were at least partly responsible for Dick's death, with their eagerness to buy whatever it was that Bryn had procured for them.

Mamie came hurrying over to Pauline and me. "Isn't this horrible?" she exclaimed. "I just can't believe it! I said to Elmer, 'Not that nice little guy!'"

His universal epitaph, I thought dully. *Here lies Dick Harvey, a nice little guy*.

"Can I get you a drink, Clare?" Morgan was at my side.

"No, thanks, I've just had one."

"Come and join us, Mr Rees." Mamie Zimmerman moved farther round the window-seat and Morgan sat down beside me.

"The police are coming," Pauline said. "What a way to end a holiday! He came here every year, you know. Mrs Davies was telling me the other day that he enjoyed the company. Outside school, I think he was rather lonely; he never mentioned any relatives."

I felt tears sting my eyes and looked down quickly. Under cover of the table, Morgan's hand closed reassuringly over mine. When I raised my head again, Philip was watching us from behind the bar. Morgan, catching our fused glances, withdrew his hand.

"Am I encroaching?" he asked quietly, as the two women chatted beside us.

"No, of course not."

"Philip mightn't agree."

I didn't reply. Whatever my own inclination, I must play by Bryn's rules, or, I thought shudderingly, I might find myself hurtling off a cliff.

"Are you sure you won't have a drink? It might help – Dick's death has shaken us all."

"No, thanks." I added sadly, "Now we'll never know what he was so excited about."

Andrew and Cindy came in and joined the group at the bar. Everyone seemed to be herding together in this small room, seeking comfort from each other. The lounge must have been empty by now except for the old ladies and the school-mistresses.

Wynne Davies returned, thanked Philip for relieving him, and took up his place again. Philip moved round to the front of the bar but made no attempt to join me. I noticed with misgiving that he'd refilled his brandy glass.

"I tried to persuade Gwynneth to go to bed, but she wouldn't," Mr Davies was saying. "It's hit her pretty hard. Like one of the family was Mr Harvey, coming here every year."

"It's dreadful." Cindy Dacombe pressed her fingers to her lips, her eyes wide to keep back the tears. Andrew's arm went comfortingly round her shoulders. "If only he'd let you go with him, Mr Mortimer," she continued. "You asked him, didn't you?"

I stiffened, striving to hear Clive's reply above the hum of conversation.

"I might have suggested it, last night," he admitted, his voice a little strained.

I thought: it would have been almost eleven when he joined me on the hill. Suppose after all he'd had access to a car? Would he have had time to drive to Pen-y-Coed and back before coming after me to establish an alibi?

Outside the window, wet darkness pressed against the panes. Was it really only nine hours since I'd sat here with Morgan, waiting for Aladdin?

As though a part of my remembering, there came the sound of a car swishing off the main road. Headlights raked the window behind us, moved on, and the long sleek car drew up at the front door.

The police had arrived.

Chapter Eight

'Can it be summed up so,
Quit in a single kiss?'

Bridges: *I will not let thee go*

WYNNE DAVIES passed the bar back to Philip and went to meet them, and a minute later Clive Mortimer, making some comment I didn't catch, followed him out of the room. We could hear voices in the hall, heavy feet moving towards the stairs, and studiously avoided each other's eyes.

The minutes went by. Though several attempts at conversation were made, we were all on edge, straining for sounds of the policemen's return.

Someone refilled my glass and I automatically drank from it. To my heightened senses, it seemed that everyone watched everyone else, trying to probe behind the masks we presented to each other. Could they guess that Philip and I were not what we seemed? Or were they equally guilty of duplicity?

I shook my head to clear it. The police were here; I'd wanted to contact them, hadn't I? Would it be possible to seize the chance to tell them what I knew? Or – I shuddered – if Dick's death really was linked with our enterprise, might they charge me with murder? Nothing, in this unreal world, seemed impossible.

After what felt like an eternity, Mr Davies reappeared in the doorway.

"The sergeant here would like to ask a couple of questions," he said, and a solid, red-faced man came forward.

"Sorry to intrude, ladies and gentlemen," he began in his lilting voice. "A nasty business, this. I wanted to ask if the deceased ever mentioned any relatives to you? It's a forlorn hope, like, since Mr and Mrs Davies here knew him better than you did, and they never heard him speak of anyone."

"There was only the school," Morgan said.

"Yes, sir, we have that address. Do any of you know where he was making for when he set off this morning, or what he'd discovered that excited him so much?"

"Not what he'd found, he was keeping it to himself." That was Elmer Zimmerman. "But as to where he was headed, surely it would have been where he was found? Wasn't his car there?"

"Yes; it was because it was still unclaimed at closing time that the alarm was raised. But, see, it's hard to think what there could have been at Pen-y-Coed to interest a man like Mr Harvey. Views and that, yes, and a lovely beach, but nothing else. And no one remembers seeing him there."

"He wasn't the sort people remember," Pauline said.

Another sad epitaph. I wished now that I'd studied Philip's map in the car; how near Cefn Fawr Castle was Pen-y-Coed?

There were a few more general questions, then the policeman took his leave. "I'll give you a receipt for his possessions, sir," he was saying, as he and Mr Davies went back through the hall.

The reflection of the brightly-lit room hung suspended in the darkness beyond the window, and I watched the people behind me mirrored in this looking-glass world, where things were the opposite of what they seemed, turning with relief as Mrs Davies came in with a tray. She was pale and red-eyed, but was quite composed.

"I've made some fresh coffee; I thought you might feel in need of it. And let's shut out this depressing darkness."

We cleared a space for the tray, and Morgan leaned over

81

to pull the heavy curtains across the bay. The room became smaller still, but cosier.

"I'll pour," I volunteered, standing up. My hand was not quite steady, but at least I didn't spill any. When everyone was served there was a cup left over, and I realised Clive Mortimer hadn't returned. I'd poured black for myself, hoping to clear my head from the lingering effects of the brandy.

Mr Davies came in, and from behind the curtained window we heard the police car drive away.

Pauline stood up. "I'll just go and make sure the children have settled. The gale was keeping them awake."

She went out. Morgan said in a low voice, "I don't suppose any of us will get much sleep tonight."

His eyes slid past me, and I turned to see Philip at my side.

"May I have a word with you, Clare? Privately?"

I hesitated, but his eyes held mine steadily.

"Excuse me a moment," I murmured to Morgan, and he rose as I left my seat. The hall felt cool after the heat in the cocktail lounge, and I shivered a little.

"What is it?"

"I've still not seen that plan. I'll come up with you now."

"If you want to look at it," I said carefully, "I'll bring it down. You're not coming to my room at this time of night. What would the old ladies think?"

He smiled unpleasantly. "Still the same, arm's length Clare? That's not what I hear from Bryn."

I said icily, "Do you want to see the plan or don't you? Can't it wait till morning?"

"No, it can't. And where *can* I look at it, then? Hardly in there."

He nodded towards the glass wall of the lounge. The old ladies must have retired to bed, but Miss Norton and Miss Bunting had pulled out a table and were engaged in some card game.

"The TV room will probably be empty."

"In here?" Philip pushed the door open. The set was switched on, but the occupants of the room were not watching it. At the sound of the door there was a flurry of arms and legs on the sofa, and little Mair, the chambermaid, her fingers fumbling at her blouse, scrambled to her feet. More slowly, the tall figure of Clive Mortimer uncoiled and rose to his.

Mair's horrified eyes went to our faces, then dropped to her feet. She said in a small, choked voice, "I'll get your coffee, sir," and slipped past us, cheeks scarlet and eyes still downcast.

Clive said amiably to Philip, "You might try knocking, old man."

He winked at me and went past us into the hall as Pauline came down the stairs. I held my breath; had she seen Mair? She paused fractionally, then came on towards us.

"Oh, there you are, Clive. Come and have your coffee."

They went together into the bar and Philip said, "So that's who you went walking with! You're certainly playing the field."

"I'll get the brochure." I ran across the hall and up the stairs. My mind was still on Clive – *could* he be Sinbad? – and I was into the bedroom before I realised firstly that the door hadn't been latched and secondly that I was not alone. The boy Evan, whose shifty eyes I'd distrusted on my arrival, turned swiftly from the bed. I had the distinct impression that his hand had been groping under the mattress.

"What are you doing?" I demanded, shrill with fright. "Why are you in my room?"

"Turning down the bed, miss. Mair's helping out downstairs this evening."

Which was one way of putting it, I thought acidly.

"Well, will you go now, please."

Only too willingly he sidled past me and out of the room. As the door closed behind him, I ran to the stool and, climbing on it, felt anxiously for the envelope, weak with relief to find it was still there. I glanced round the room, wondering where

83

else Evan's searching fingers had intruded. The few valuables I had with me – a gold chain and bracelet – I was wearing, and a quick check showed nothing appeared to be missing. Perhaps I'd disturbed him just in time. I resolved to lock everything away in my suitcase in future.

When I returned downstairs, Philip was standing in the television lounge, staring at the set.

"Close the door," he said without turning round. I did so.

"Evan was in my room," I told him unevenly. "I think he was feeling under the mattress."

Philip turned then, his eyes going to the brochure in my hand. "He didn't find it."

"No. You think that's what he was looking for?"

Philip shrugged. "Search me. Now, sit down." He gestured towards the sofa, but I made my way over to a chair. He stopped me, none too gently.

"Don't be a bloody fool, Clare, I'm not going to molest you. We have to look at the thing together, for God's sake!"

Stiffly I seated myself at one end of the sofa. The cushions were still warm and dented from the previous occupants. Philip sat down beside me, took the plan out of my hands and spread it over both our laps.

"I thought you said it was marked?"

"I rubbed it out, as instructed. It was there." I laid my finger on the spot.

"Looks like a long stone passage. What's the description of the castle?" He ran his finger quickly down the printed lines. *"Site might have been occupied by the Romans . . . Rhys ab Tewdwr* – Where are we? Ah – *set round a small courtyard – solar at the west end of the hall.* Here we are . . . *a long corridor formed by a natural fissure in the rock. This extends almost two hundred feet and is lit by spy holes cut in the rock."*

I bent forward to look more closely, and, as my hair brushed against his face, heard his indrawn breath. "Still wearing *Cabochard*, I notice."

"You've got the final directions, haven't you?"

He laughed shortly. "Down, Fido! Yes, I have them: four paces from the ninth spy hole, on the wall opposite. The stone with a chip out of it is loose and, surprise, surprise, it pulls out."

"And it – they fit in there?"

"Easily. They're in cardboard tubes."

Drugs, diamonds, in cardboard tubes?

I said, "How deep is the cavity?"

"Oh, the walls are eight feet thick in places – never less than four. They knew how to build in those days. Well, we'll find out tomorrow how the land lies. We need to establish what security measures are taken at night, how close in we can take the car, and so on. Then, all systems go for Beanstalk."

But tomorrow Goldilocks would come. In all the tumult of the day, I kept forgetting that. What would happen when there were two of us? And for her part, if no one approached her, she'd lose no time contacting Bryn. How could I have imagined I would get away with this?

I gazed unseeingly at the flickering screen, thinking of the red-faced sergeant who'd just left. Had Dick's death really barred me from going to the police? And what would happen to Philip – and, through him, to Matthew – if I did?

Yet if I didn't, I myself could be in danger. Even if I helped Philip retrieve whatever it was, sooner or later they'd discover I wasn't Goldilocks. Then what? If they *had* killed Dick Harvey, it was an indication of how highly they valued their operation. I wondered detachedly if Philip would let them kill me.

Turning my head, I found him watching me. As our eyes met, he said briskly, "Well, that's all. You'd better go."

Still bewildered by my musings, I said blankly, "Go where?"

"Out of this room – anywhere." He stood up. "Your admirers will be waiting impatiently in the bar."

I flushed. "There's no need to be offensive."

"I assure you I could have put it far more crudely. But if you will wear dresses like that, and perfume like that, and look – like that – you must be prepared to take the consequences."

I stood up, the unfolded plan dangling from my hands. "I've no idea what you're talking about." My voice was shaking.

"Then go, before you find out."

His eyes, hard and unwavering, held mine, and in the stillness between us, the door handle rattled suddenly. In a panic my eyes dropped to the booklet. Where could I hide it in the split-second left to me?

I'd half turned towards the sofa, but Philip moved faster. In one movement he pulled me swiftly towards him, the incriminating map concealed between us, and his mouth came down on mine.

And this was nothing like his old, milk-and-water kisses that had made me sleepily romantic after tennis club dances. This was neat alcohol. I gasped, lost my breath, but his grip didn't slacken. Behind us the door had opened and, after a moment, gently closed, and still he went on kissing me, roughly and ruthlessly, as though punishing me somehow for being what he thought I was.

Finally he released me, turning away so abruptly that the map fell unheeded to the floor. My hands went to my bruised mouth. I said stupidly, "Philip!" and he gave a harsh laugh.

"That surprised you, didn't it? Is that how Bryn kisses you? No – don't answer that, I don't want to know. You should have gone when I told you. For God's sake go now."

I went. Out in the hall, I put a hand to my face and found my cheeks were wet. I leant back against the door, helplessly wiping away the tears and trying to stop the weakening, bone-melting shaking that possessed me.

A voice said, "Miss Laurie – is something wrong?"

I turned to meet the concerned eyes of Andrew Dacombe, and tried to smile.

"Everything's been a bit of a shock, that's all." I prayed he'd think I meant Dick Harvey.

"I know. Mrs Davies brought us fresh coffee, if you'd like to come to the lounge. It might help to steady you."

Since my own cup had been left, barely tasted, in the cocktail bar, I let him take my arm and lead me across the hall, wondering dully who had opened the door and seen me with Philip.

The school-teachers, having put away their cards, were talking to Cindy, and Mair was in the act of removing the cold coffee urn. Her face reddened when she saw me, and she hurried out, avoiding my eyes.

"What's the matter with the girl?" Miss Bunting inquired, blinking nervously. "She seems very much on edge tonight."

"We all are, my dear," boomed Miss Norton.

Joan Bunting flushed. "Oh dear, how stupid of me!"

"I'll pour," I said, for the second time in fifteen minutes, glad to have something to occupy me. My hand was no steadier than before, but no one made any comment. Andrew switched on the electric fire which stood in the hearth.

"Ah, that's better, Mr Dacombe!" Miss Norton drew her chair closer. She was still wearing that terrible puce.

Cindy said, "It's starting to get cooler in the evenings, isn't it?"

"It's hardly evening, my dear; must be at least eleven o'clock."

"That late?" Miss Bunting twittered. "I hadn't realised; I hope the coffee won't keep me awake."

"Everyone's delaying going up tonight," Andrew said, his comic clown's face serious.

"And to think," Miss Norton intoned, "that only last evening, poor Mr Harvey was sitting where you are now, Joan."

Miss Bunting jumped nervously and looked behind her.

"No man knoweth of his sepulchre!" said Miss Norton with relish.

"Oh, please don't!" Cindy protested. She sounded close to tears.

Andrew said quickly, "I was fascinated to hear of your

research, Miss Norton. Do you travel all round the world in search of fairy stories?"

I swallowed the hot coffee, my mind spinning. *Andrew?* Was this return to the subject for my benefit, or was he simply changing the conversation? I hadn't seriously considered him as Sinbad, but perhaps that was a mistake.

"Not, I fear, on a teacher's salary, Mr Dacombe," Miss Norton was saying. "But during the holidays—"

As he politely listened to her, I studied him more carefully – the red-brown hair that wouldn't lie flat, the short nose and flared nostrils, the wide mouth. Not, surely, the face of a murderer? For if Dick Harvey's death had indeed been deliberate, it must surely be Sinbad who was responsible.

Cindy stood up and laid her cup and saucer on the tray, her pony-tail swinging over her shoulder as she bent forward, her long, bare legs glowing redly in the light from the fire.

Could she be Goldilocks? I thought suddenly, as everyone's identity shifted in my mind yet again. If Bryn was as devious as Philip said, perhaps it wasn't 'the Lawrence girl' after all.

Cindy – Cinderella—

"I think I'll go up, darling," she was saying. "Somebody's got to make a move."

Andrew nodded and got to his feet.

"So will I," I said, unwilling to be left with the schoolmistresses, and in any case anxious for this troubled and confusing day to end.

I followed them up the stairs, said good-night as we turned in opposite directions, and went into my room. At least this time it was empty.

I stopped suddenly. The brochure! I was supposed to be in charge of that! Had Philip got it? I'd been in no condition to think of it when I'd stumbled from the room. Suppose it had been kicked under the sofa and he'd forgotten it too?

I turned and ran quickly back down the stairs. The door to

the television lounge was open and I ran straight in before I realised that someone had beaten me to it. Andrew Dacombe, whom I'd just left upstairs, turned quickly at my approach. For a moment we stared at each other. Then he said,

"Forgotten something?"

"I – can't find my hanky. I thought perhaps—"

"Sorry, I haven't seen it. Well, good-night again."

"Good-night," I echoed, watching him go from the room. It was hardly worth looking now; if the pamphlet had been here, Andrew would have found it. He'd seen me leave this room earlier – was that why he'd come back?

I shivered, uneasy at being alone down here. Quickly I ran my hand under the sofa and then, with an eye on the open door, felt between the heavy cushions. Nothing. I could only hope Philip had it, but there was no way I was going to ask him tonight.

I turned and almost ran from the room. Voices still came from the bar – perhaps Morgan was waiting there with my undrunk cup of coffee – but the lounge lights were off now. I ran on up the stairs.

Almost in my ear, a voice said, "Good-night, my dear!"

I whirled with an involuntary cry, to see Miss Hettie – or Miss Olwen – the light was too dim to distinguish any brooch – smiling at me. One thick grey plait hung over her shoulder, a horrible travesty, to my tortured mind, of Cindy's golden pony-tail. Youth and age.

The old lady nodded to me and continued on her way, her sponge-bag in her hand.

"Good-night," I stammered belatedly, "Miss—"

"Hettie," she supplied, and added as she closed the door, "the younger one."

With shaking fingers I began to undress, and had just slipped on my dressing-gown when there was a tap at the door.

Instantly I froze, all the fears of the previous night sluicing over me as I gazed, mesmerised, at the knob, waiting for it to turn. It did not, and after a minute the tap came again, accompanied by Miss Norton's voice.

"Miss Laurie? You're not in bed already?"

The breath tearing at my lungs, I unsnipped the door and opened it a crack. She was standing smiling at me, a thick book in her hand.

"Sorry to disturb you, but I thought this might provide some bedtime reading. Volume One, as promised. I hope you find it interesting."

I reached out to take it. "Thank you, I'm – sure I shall."

She nodded. "Good-night to you, then."

I closed and relocked the door, clutching the heavy book against me, and as my chaotic breathing quietened, sat down on the bed and opened it.

Unfortunately, my initial interest soon waned; though the subject was undeniably fascinating, the style of writing was so heavy and ponderous that I decided unfairly the only way it would form part of my bedtime reading would be as a substitute for sleeping pills.

Laying it on the table, I climbed into bed and switched off the light.

Chapter Nine

'The splendour falls on castle walls . . .'

Tennyson: *The Princess*

SOMEHOW, the night passed. The events of the day, which surely must have been the longest I had lived through, circled endlessly in my head: my walk on the hill with Clive; waiting for Aladdin and meeting Philip; the miserable afternoon at the beach, the news about Dick Harvey and, finally, the trauma of Philip's kiss. It was this last which was uppermost in my mind.

At length I flicked on the light and poured myself a glass of water. The hands on my little clock pointed reproachfully to ten past three. I drank the whole glassful in small, cold sips while I tried to reason with myself.

Philip's opinion of me was unchanged. I was, like him, an accessory to some sort of crime, hand-in-glove with the leader; the kind of girl to whom one kiss more or less was of little consequence – and his prime concern, let it be remembered, had been to conceal the brochure.

It was also as well to remind myself that he was himself 'up to the neck in this unsavoury business', as he'd accused me of being. So, I reasoned, if this hostile, cold-eyed stranger had stirred me more with one brutal kiss than his counterpart had in over four years of gentleness, then that was my bad luck, and the sooner I forgot about it, the better.

I snapped off the light with a little click of finality, lay down again, and willed sleep to come. Eventually, it did.

It was cooler in the morning after all the rain, and I selected a pale yellow jumper and matching linen skirt. Today we were going to storm the castle, and dank stone corridors are apt to be chill.

Before going down to breakfast I shook out the dress I'd worn the previous evening and hung it in the wardrobe, leaving exposed on the chair the sweater Philip had lent me in the storm.

I picked it up carefully, as though it might bite me. It was still a little damp and smelled faintly of after-shave, and I put it hastily back on the chair. I could give it to him after breakfast; first, I had to face the ordeal of meeting him again, after our parting the night before.

I checked in the mirror that my two disturbed nights did not call for additional make-up, but I looked remarkably well. Only the shadows under my eyes, which I'd brought with me from London, had still not disappeared.

Philip was already in the dining-room, reading a Sunday newspaper. Dick Harvey's table, which yesterday had borne the marmalade-smeared plate, was bare. I averted my eyes as I went to join Philip. He stood up and pulled out my chair, his eyes wary.

"You're like an advertisement for instant sunshine."

"I wish I felt like it." I had not meant to sound bitter.

"Didn't you sleep well?"

"Not very."

"Up to tackling the task in hand?"

"I've no option, have I?"

"The sun will probably break through later. I've ordered packed lunches, by the way, since we didn't get a chance to last night."

Morgan, overhearing this as he passed our table, stopped and cocked an eyebrow. "A shade optimistic, aren't you? It's quite likely to bucket down again."

"Then we'll eat in the car. I think Clare should get away for the day; hotels aren't the most cheerful places on Sundays, and this week it'll be even worse." His eyes flicked to the empty table.

"No doubt you're right. Well, I hope it keeps fine for you."

He moved on. Round the dining-room the tables began to fill up, and as I observed the strained eyes and pale faces of our fellow guests, I began to be glad we'd be away all day, even if I was less than comfortable in Philip's company.

His voice cut into my musings. "As you probably noticed, I had rather more to drink last night than I should have done."

I looked up. If that was meant as an apology, it was one I could have done without.

I forced myself to speak lightly. "No problem. You have got the booklet, haven't you?"

He nodded.

"I panicked when I remembered it. In fact, I ran back to look for it, but—"

I broke off as Harry approached with the coffee, and for the rest of the meal no further reference was made to the subject uppermost in both our minds.

Our packed lunches were awaiting us on the reception desk.

"I'll get my mac," I said.

I met Mair on the landing and handed her Philip's sweater to dry off. She said in a low voice, "I'm sorry, miss, about last night."

"It's nothing to do with me, Mair."

"No, miss, but I was that ashamed. You won't say anything, will you? To Mrs Mortimer, I mean?"

"Of course not, but for her sake rather than yours."

Mair hung her head. "It was proper wicked. It won't happen again, miss."

I left her with her guilty conscience and went downstairs, the mac over my arm. Philip had gone outside and was waiting for me by the car.

"I wonder if Clive *is* Sinbad?" I mused as we drove out of the hotel gateway. "He could have persuaded Mair to lend him my key so he could leave the note."

"But what possible reason could he have given? Far too risky. Anyway, he can't be Sinbad – he's too busy being Bluebeard!"

I smiled in spite of myself.

"Frankly," Philip added, "I don't understand your obsession with Sinbad. What does it matter who he is? We'll find out soon enough."

I subsided quickly. True, to Philip it wouldn't matter, and it shouldn't to Goldilocks, either.

The morning was crystal clear, the grey-blue sky an inverted bowl from which all the cloud and rain had been spilled. But the metaphorical storms were only just gathering; today, the real Goldilocks would come, and with her, the danger of detection.

"Andrew was pumping Miss Norton about fairy tales last night," I said. "I wondered if it was for my benefit. Then, as I started to tell you, when I went back to look for the brochure, I found him in the TV lounge."

"There you go again! If he *is* Sinbad, he knows as much as we do, if not more, so he wouldn't need to snoop around. You're making things needlessly complicated; the poor man probably went in to watch TV!"

"But he'd just gone up to bed," I said a little sulkily. "You don't think there could be a rival gang of some kind?"

"Don't be ridiculous."

We had turned off the main valley road and now the landscape was falling away on either side to reveal wider vistas. I settled back to enjoy the drive. The road threaded its way past deserted pit-heads, black and ugly against the skyline like the humps of old Welsh dragons, and on through twisting narrow streets between stone cottages that had belonged to the miners. A group of children stood in a doorway licking iced lollies, the faded cotton of their dresses splashes of colour against the drab stone.

Then up and out on to the open road again, narrowly avoiding a suicidal sheep. Now we began to climb and Philip changed gear, hugging the left-hand verge. On our side of the road, thickly wooded slopes rose steeply, but on the right a sheer drop fell away to the valley below. Above the noise of the car, I could hear the rush of running water, and guessed that a waterfall must be hurling itself over the edge into a river hundreds of feet beneath us.

Gradually, as we descended again, the drop on the right became less lethal, and we entered a wide, smiling valley dotted with picture-book farmhouses. Hens clucked contentedly by the roadside and dogs lay in the sun which now, as Philip had forecast, was beginning to break through. And all around us, like a protective embrace, fold after fold of hills overlapped each other, stretching away into the blue distance.

I stirred and felt him glance at me. It was at least twenty minutes since either of us had spoken.

"Spectacular, isn't it?"

I nodded and stretched, swivelling in my seat to follow the flight of a jay which rose suddenly from a hedge. But my attention was diverted from its progress by the sight of a small red car on the road behind us. I remembered seeing a similar one some time before, and felt a prickle of unease.

I said – and my voice was unnaturally loud – "We're not being followed, are we?"

His eyes went to the mirror. "I don't think so. I noticed him a while back, but this is a public road, after all, and there haven't been many places he could have turned off."

I was only partly reassured. The road plunged down into a small wood, a long green tunnel where the branches met overhead. I sat quietly, watching the bars of sunlight flick across the road. The first leaves were starting to turn gold, seeming sun-kissed even in the shadows. We climbed up out of the wood and the road straightened.

Philip said, "We should be able to see the castle soon. Yes, look – over there."

I followed the direction of his finger. Away in the distance, Cefn Fawr dominated the surrounding countryside from its great height. Its grey stone prismed the sunshine into a thousand refractions, so that it glittered like a fairy palace, its twin towers outlined dramatically against the now deep blue of the sky behind it.

"It's beautiful," I said in a hushed tone.

"And dangerous, to those who try to storm it."

It was a timely reminder. I wished vehemently that we needn't approach any nearer the fairy castle. I wanted to remember it as it looked at this moment, ethereal, a fragment of the past dreaming in the sunshine, with the wide, safe spaces of the valley separating it from us.

"Do we have to go?" I asked in a small voice.

"Cold feet, Clare? At this stage?"

"But suppose someone sees us – on Tuesday, I mean? Is it really worth all the risks involved?"

"That's a question you should have asked Bryn before you set out. Personally, I'd have thought a couple of million is worth a few risks, even if we get only a fraction of it."

A wave of shock sluiced over me, and I only just bit back an exclamation as I realised for the first time the enormity of what I'd stumbled into. I licked dry lips.

"Is that the price they put on it?"

"It's what the company had to fork out."

The company? *Matthew's* company? I couldn't ask.

I said weakly, "Yes – yes, I was forgetting."

We were both silent, and the only sound was the hum of the wheels on the hard surface of the road. I felt a little sick; if indeed Matthew's firm was involved, it must be a very personal vendetta Philip was engaged in. But it would be better not to pursue that line of thought.

To distract myself, I glanced in the wing mirror. The red car was still behind us, but as Philip said, there'd been no turning it could have taken.

Ahead of us, Cefn Fawr was now much nearer. On top of its

promontory it seemed to grow out of the rock itself, and must command a view of many miles, to sea as well as over the land. On the side we were approaching the rock rose murderously sheer, with, as far as I could see, no cracks or crevices to give foothold. And Philip and I had to storm it and steal a treasure from its vaults. I shivered apprehensively.

"Bryn never said it would be easy," Philip remarked drily, "but he had the tougher job, hiding them there in the first place."

He drew in to the side of the road and took out a large-scale map. "While I think of it, I want to check the best route to Swansea."

"Swansea?" I echoed blankly.

He glanced at me in surprise. "To the boat."

"Oh," I said lamely. "Yes, of course."

"I've got a packing case in the boot, and once clear of the castle we'll load the rolls into it and batten it down. It's identical to all the others that'll be in the hold.

"Right, this is the road we're on, and we're now about – here." His finger was tracing the map and I leant over to follow it. "After another mile or so we turn off on to this road, which, as you can see, is a dead end leading only to the castle. Presumably there's some kind of parking area at the foot of the hill, but it won't be much good to us at dead of night; we need to get in much closer."

"But there aren't any other roads down there."

"Precisely, so we'll have to bump the car up a sheep-track or something. That's the point of this trip; we must know exactly where we're making for when the time comes.

"Our chief worry is not to have to carry the rolls too far. It's not that they're particularly heavy, but they *are* cumbersome, and even though there are nine of them, we daren't risk going back a second time. Which, of course, is why Bryn decreed you should accompany me." He turned to look at me. "Though I wish to hell he hadn't. Look, Clare, whatever you've done up to now, this is no job for you. It could be big trouble.

For Matthew's sake, will you leave it to me? I can manage somehow, and Bryn need never know."

I said steadily, "It would be more dangerous for you alone, wouldn't it?"

"The hell with that."

I shook my head. "No, Philip, I'll go with you. It's what I'm here for."

I thought he was going to argue, but if so, he changed his mind and returned to the map with an offhand, "On your own head, then.

"Now, once we've retrieved them and returned to the car, we rejoin this road we're on now and follow it for ten miles or so. We turn off here, on to this B road, and from there we can drop down, thank God, to join the M4 for the last few miles. It'll take a good hour; did you check on the tides?"

"No, not yet. It all sounds rather terrifying."

"Not really; we shouldn't run into any trouble. No one will be guarding the rolls, because no one knows they're there. It's most unlikely there'll be any hitch, but if there is, the alternative plan will slide smoothly into operation. Bryn leaves nothing to chance, as you should know."

"How do we explain being out so late when we get back to the hotel?"

"Why do you think there's all this build-up about our relationship?"

"I'd have thought it would be possible, and a lot more comfortable, to conduct it at the hotel, without staying out half the night."

"An interesting point," Philip said drily. I felt my cheeks grow hot.

"And what happens when we get to the docks?" I asked hurriedly.

"We hand over the packing case to Rumpelstiltskin – why *did* Bryn choose these ridiculous names? – after which we make a quick exit. Then it's just a straightforward journey back along the M4, off at the Dryffyd junction, and so to the hotel."

"By which time the door will be locked and everyone convinced we've also fallen off some convenient cliff."

"Perhaps. But we knock them up with profuse apologies about flat tyres and running out of petrol, which we don't really expect anyone to believe."

"Charming," I said sarcastically.

"So now" – he closed the map and pushed it back under the dashboard "—we spy out the land a bit more closely. What happened to the red car, by the way? Did you notice?"

"It passed us when we stopped. There was nothing else it could do."

In fact, while we'd been poring over the map there'd been a noticeable increase in traffic, and as we reached the junction with its sign to the castle, several other cars coming from the other direction also turned off. I relaxed a little. It was a sunny Sunday in the middle of the tourist season, and no doubt the red Austin was as innocent as all the rest of them.

We parked in the designated area and while Philip locked the car, I turned to look up at the castle. And it was at that moment that a cloud slid across the face of the sun. The effect was instant and dramatic; with the removal of its light the fortress loomed over us, suddenly sinister, a brooding pile some nine hundred years old. My foreboding returned in full measure.

Philip, however, had turned from the castle to the hill on our right, a more gentle gradient covered for the most part in grass.

"I think it would be an idea to go up there first," he said. "We could study the layout better at a slight distance and might spot some alternative approach."

I nodded, only too thankful to postpone visiting the castle, and we crossed the road and started up the bank. Here the ground rose gradually, the grey-green, brittle grass an obvious haunt of sheep. Philip took my arm to help me over the rough part, and the naturalness of the gesture made my heart ache.

I didn't want to think, yet, of the way my feelings were developing towards him. I knew only that my old half-impatient, half-affectionate attitude had been swept away by something altogether stronger and, in the circumstances, more dangerous. It seemed impossible that he could be so different now from what he'd always been, when I'd thought I knew him so well.

We stopped on a little bluff to get our breath.

"A penny for them, Clare?"

"I was thinking," I said reluctantly, "that you've changed."

"Not really."

"You were always a hard-bitten criminal?" I kept my voice light, afraid to let the conversation become personal, but he steered it skilfully back.

"I was always considerably tougher than you realised, if that's what you mean."

"But you seem – older," I said.

"So do you, Clare. More mature, somehow. No doubt I have Bryn to thank for that." His voice hardened. "He hasn't hurt you in any way?"

I shook my head wordlessly.

"And you really love him?"

"Please, Philip!" I turned my face away.

"What's the harm in telling me? I always knew you didn't give a damn for me."

I was too shaken to attempt a denial. "You did?"

"It was obvious. No strings, no pressure of any kind. That's not the way a girl behaves when she's in love. Everything had to be light and superficial, so I tried to keep it that way, though it was one hell of a strain at times. But there you are, I was a fool. If you'd asked me to stand on my head, I'd have done it."

We were standing side by side staring out to sea, an opaque expanse under the cloudy sky, and I was grateful I didn't have to look at him. I felt confused, uncertain, being forced to look at myself through his eyes, and not liking what I saw, wanting to stop this painful dissection, but incapable of doing so.

"Matthew tried to warn me," Philip went on. "He told me I gave in to you too much, that you'd get tired of always having your own way, but I couldn't see it. I was afraid that if I stopped being easy and compliant, I should lose you."

I swallowed, made myself speak. "If you knew I didn't love you, why ask me to marry you?"

He shrugged, his hands deep in his trouser pockets. "You weren't interested in anyone else. I reckoned that if you were prepared to marry me, I'd more than enough love for both of us.

"But of course, Matthew was right – I should have realised he knew you better than I ever would. You got bored very quickly, didn't you, though for a time you were too polite to show it. It was only after your parents' deaths that things went badly wrong. Time and again, when I longed to comfort you, it was only Matthew you wanted, and it soon became clear that I was getting on your nerves.

"So" – he lifted his shoulders – "you threw caution to the winds and moved to the flat. I knew then it was over, though I still wouldn't admit it. Not until – everything blew. And that was the perfect excuse, wasn't it – might have been tailor-made. You were able to let me swing with a clear conscience."

I said shakily, "Please, Philip—"

"And of course, by that time there was Bryn. I can see the attraction he must have had for you – dark, intense, the very antithesis of me. As you were at pains to point out yesterday."

He turned suddenly, surprising the tears on my face. "Don't cry, Clare. It's past history, and I've learned my lesson. I shall never let myself be that vulnerable again."

Past history for him, but only just starting for me. How shallow and selfish I'd been, using him for my own ends and discarding him with relief when he needed me most.

I said, and the effort of speaking at all tore at my throat, "How you must hate me."

"No," he contradicted quietly, "I've never hated you, though I came pretty near it yesterday, when I saw you waiting in the bar. Come on now, dry your eyes. There's nothing to be gained from a post-mortem at this stage – I don't know why I embarked on it. The past is well and truly over. For the record, are you going to marry Bryn?"

"No!" I said violently.

"Perhaps you're right; he's not the marrying kind. Well, after all that, are you ready to go on?"

I nodded. He didn't take my arm and we climbed stiffly, separately, my hands in fists against my sides. The sun had come out again, but I hardly noticed. The salt wind lifted my hair and blew it in a cloud across my face. In it, I could detect a lingering memory of the perfume I'd worn the night before – Philip's *Cabochard*.

We stopped again and turned to look back the way we had come. We were now almost on a level with the castle opposite, and its time-worn battlements faced us, grey and forbidding, across the intervening space. It struck me that we were studying it with much the same calculation as its enemies of old had done. How many of them had succeeded in storming it?

Below us, in the dip, we could see the collection of parked cars, our own among them. Just beyond them, at the foot of the path up to the castle, stood a small, white-washed cottage with some kind of table outside, round which half a dozen people were milling. The path itself was dotted along its length with tiny, bent figures, but our searching eyes could discern no other approach to the castle.

"The corridor must be on the sea side," Philip remarked, his eyes narrowed against the sun. He was staring across, his fair hair blowing in the wind, his body braced, hard and firm, against it, and I felt a surge of irreparable loss such as I'd known when my parents were killed. He'd been mine, and I'd let him slip through my fingers. On cue, the words of a song

102

my mother used to sing came into my head: *Careless hands, that can't hold on to love.*

I held my own hands straight out in front of me, looking down at them. They were long and slim and brown, and the circle of Philip's ring was no longer discernible. *Careless hands don't care when dreams slip through.*

"What on earth are you doing?" His amused voice broke into my introspection.

"Nothing," I said, self-consciously putting my hands behind me.

"Well, we might as well go down. I can't see anything from this side that will be of any help."

It was easier going downhill and we reached the car fairly quickly.

"Let's take an apple each to eat on the climb." He unlocked the door and rummaged in the packages lying on the back seat. I wished dully we could get in and drive away without going near the castle, but Philip, apparently sharing none of my misgivings, had already relocked the door and was walking towards the cottage. I fell into step beside him.

As we drew nearer, I saw that on the table outside it were piles of postcards and pamphlets such as that passed to me by Sinbad, and the woman in charge was doing a brisk trade.

"You have got the brochure?" I asked belatedly, biting into the sweet, crisp fruit.

"Yes, in my pocket. We needn't waste money on another."

Ahead of us a family with two children were already starting the ascent. The smaller child at once started to whine, and her father scooped her up and set off up the slope bearing her on his shoulders. Two other couples who had been purchasing brochures fell in behind us. As Sinbad had directed, we were now surrounded by ordinary holidaymakers; if only our presence here was as innocuous as theirs.

"How long will you stay on," I asked Philip, "after Tuesday?"

"No longer than I can help. I'll catch up on my sleep on

103

Wednesday and start for home the next day. What about
you? No doubt you'll be wanting to get back and report to
Bryn. It must be one hell of a strain for him, having to keep
his distance, but he couldn't be seen near the Zimmermans.
I must say, though, I'm surprised that Carol's not here."

"Carol?" I said sharply.

"Carol Lawrence. After all, it was her baby."

So I'd been right the first time: Carol Lawrence was Goldilocks. Of course – Bryn had asked for her when he phoned
the Plas Dinas. 'Miss Lawrence, is it?' Gareth had said, and
I'd led him on to my own name.

We had reached the point where the proper ascent began.
Philip flung his apple core into the long grass and looked up
the steep path ahead of us. "Ready?"

I drew a deep breath. "Ready," I echoed.

"Then – excelsior!"

Side by side, we set off for the castle.

Chapter Ten

'Look here upon this picture, and on this;'
                              Shakespeare: *Hamlet*

FROM the beginning, the going was harder on this side and for some time, intent on the climb, neither of us spoke. We had overtaken the couple with the children and there was no one within earshot when Philip remarked suddenly, "I hope they haven't got a dog at that cottage; it might bark at an awkward moment."

"That would be all we need."

He flung me a mocking, sideways glance. "Cheer up, Clare, remember you're doing this for love!"

"Well, you're certainly not," I retorted. "Why *are* you doing it, Philip?"

"Just for the hell of it, I suppose. The element of risk, outwitting authority."

"Not to mention," I added spitefully, "defrauding the insurance companies, in other words your step-father. Your own personal revenge."

"How very astute of you, dear Clare." His voice was light enough, but there was a dangerous undercurrent. That, I realised, was what he'd meant about my hurting Matthew; I hadn't known, then, that insurance was involved.

The track twisted and looped its way up the steep hillside, bringing us ever nearer to the ancient battlements towering above us until, rounding the final bend, we saw the gateway directly ahead – the entrance to the castle.

I paused, holding my side and gasping for breath after the steep climb. Philip ran a hand testingly over the heavy hinge and looked at his fingers. "Oil," he said softly. "Well maintained – it must be closed every night."

"You'd think," I remarked acidly, "that after resisting the Normans and Cromwell, it wouldn't have too much trouble keeping us out."

Philip opened the booklet and read aloud. "*This magnificent fortress, standing four hundred feet high and surrounded on three sides by steep, almost vertical precipices, could be taken only by surprise or by starvation.*

"I plump for surprise. It's in a state of ruin anyway – we could easily climb over some of these walls."

"With a four-hundred foot drop below?"

"On this side, you goose."

"Morning sir, miss." A peak-capped figure ambled towards us. "That'll be one-fifty each, if you please. Grand day after yesterday, isn't it?"

"It is indeed," Philip answered pleasantly. "I suppose rain's not very good for business?"

The man shook his head. "Had to close early. A blow, that, slap in the middle of the busy season."

"What time are you usually open till?"

"Five-thirty, sir."

He touched his cap and moved on to the couple who'd come up behind us.

"Gatehouse on the left, guard-room on the right," Philip murmured, referring to the plan. "I think our passage must be over there. It looks as though we have to go down some steps."

I said quickly, "Well, now we're here, we might as well see everything else first."

He lifted an eyebrow. "Playing the tourist, are we?"

"As instructed," I reminded him. "I meant to ask when you had the map out: how far is Pen-y-Coed from here?"

106

"Five or six miles up the coast." He glanced at me. "Let's be logical about this. *If* this was where Harvey made his discovery, and he came back to check it the next day, why would he waste time going on to Pen-y-Coed? Surely his most likely course would be either to hot-foot it back to the hotel and a phone, or drive to Cardiff or Swansea to report the find in person. You said he mentioned contacting the authorities."

"But he was found at Pen-y-Coed," I said stubbornly.

"Exactly. Which to my mind means he was never here at all. There's not a shred of evidence to prove he was, nor, for that matter, that his death wasn't accidental. For my money, he dug up some sort of artefact, perhaps in a cave on the cliffs, and when he returned to re-examine it, he slipped, lost his footing, and fell to his death."

Admittedly it sounded plausible, and I wished I could believe it. I'd much prefer Dick's death to have been an accident rather than a deliberate act of violence.

Continuing our exploration, we wandered through an archway into what had once been the Great Hall. Stone steps, hollowed in the centre by centuries of wear, led at one end to a ruined gallery, opposite which was the remains of an enormous chimney. I went over to the deep window embrasure and looked through the slit-like opening at the sunlit hillside.

Below me, the rocks on this northern face fell sheer and steep, while to the right fields spread out to the horizon. In one of them, minute in the distance, a tractor was at work. On my left, far below, lay the flat brown sands of low tide.

I turned to find Philip beside me. "Except for the tractor," I commented, "the view can't have changed much over the centuries. It's easy to imagine them here, keeping watch for the approach of the enemy."

"Well, the enemy is now within," Philip said shortly. "Come on, we can't put it off any longer; let's have a look at that corridor."

I sighed, turning reluctantly from the peaceful scene. The castle, magnificent even in its crumbling decay, depressed me.

We returned to the courtyard and walked over to the far corner. Nearby, the family with the children were posing while the father took a photograph.

Philip said, "I'll go first. Watch your step."

I followed him through the low entrance and down a flight of steps, and at once a dank, cold smell came to meet us, redolent of the past. On our right, a series of spy-holes provided the only source of light, directing their narrow beams on to the wall opposite, where they were all but absorbed by the damp stone. Philip started to count the apertures under his breath.

"There are more steps halfway along," he warned over his shoulder. "They're bound to be slippery, and the rock even here is worn and uneven. Take care how you go."

Cautiously, hands pressing against the walls for support, I went after him.

"Here are the steps now."

He started down them and I followed. But despite my caution, my foot slid on a treacherous piece of rock, and before I could regain my balance, I'd hurtled down the remaining few steps, coming up hard against Philip. He caught my arms, holding me like a vice pressed tightly against him. Then, as I righted myself, his hands fell away.

"Did you hurt yourself?" He was breathing quickly.

"No. Sorry if I winded you; I lost my footing."

"Don't twist your ankle, for God's sake – it's lethal down here. I'm not surprised everyone else is giving it a miss. All right to go on? That spy-hole is the sixth – three to go. You'd better take my hand."

I did so, feeling his fingers tighten round mine. The little round holes were still appearing at regular intervals on our right. I peered through one as we passed, but all that was visible was sky and sea.

"Eight," Philip counted, "nine. Now, one – two – three – four paces." He stopped, and I of necessity with him. "Nobody behind us, is there?"

I looked back up the dark, echoing passage to the square of light at the far end. "Not a soul."

"Keep your ears pricked." He felt in his pocket for a torch, flicked it on, and bent to the left-hand wall. Then he gave a quick exclamation.

My heart did a somersault. "What is it?"

"Someone *has* been here; the edge of the stone's proud, look – it's not been completely pushed back." He straightened, meeting my eyes. "Could be you were right after all. I'd better check; we don't want to go through all the rigmarole, only to find the cupboard is bare."

I said quickly, "No, Philip, don't touch it – it's too risky. Someone could come in any minute – let's go back."

"But dammit I have to look. If Harvey *was* here, he could have moved them somewhere else for safety, in which case we might as well pack our bags and go home."

I stared at him, and he added succinctly, "We wouldn't have a hope of finding them, would we, now he's been done away with?"

Been done away with. The phrase echoed ominously in my head. So now Philip accepted it, too. His fingers were scrabbling under the rock and slowly, surely, it began to inch out from the wall.

"I'm not sure how heavy this is." His voice came back to me, resounding against the dank stone. "Can you take one end?"

I slid my hands under the emerging slab and its ancient chill struck through to the core of my body. I shuddered.

"Hang on, Clare. Soon be – out – in the sunshine – again."

He staggered against me as the stone came away, revealing a dark cavity. "Lower your end to the floor – gently – and we'll prop it against the far wall."

The task completed, we turned to peer into the hole.

"It goes back for miles," I said.

Philip flicked the torch again. "At least some of them are still here, but I'll have to do a quick count. God, look – this one's been tampered with!"

He reached inside and pulled out a cardboard tube some three feet long. The polythene which had enclosed it had been torn back, and the exposed cardboard felt cold and slightly damp.

"Make sure it's still inside, while I count the rest."

He shoved the tube at me and turned back to the cavity. I was actually holding it, the key to the whole business.

Breathing quickly, I stood the tube upright and felt gingerly inside. A roll of canvas, I thought, as my fingers made contact. Cautiously, my heart beating high in my chest, I tugged it a few inches clear and carefully turned it back. In the dim light from the spy-holes something glowed vibrantly – rich, velvety red, midnight blue and emerald.

With held breath I swivelled the tube on the floor and cautiously started to unroll the canvas, gasping as my eyes met other eyes – gentle, painted eyes in the face of a Madonna.

"Is it still inside?" Philip asked without turning, his voice echoing in the hollow rock.

"Yes," I whispered, "it's here."

"Thank God for that."

Reverently I slid my precious discovery back into the tube, pulling the torn outer cover round it as best I could.

"They're all accounted for, then. God, what a relief! Give it to me." He reached out and I put the tube into his hand, my mind whirling furiously. Who did these masterpieces belong to? Had some major art gallery been robbed?

"Right, give me a hand with the slab again."

Mechanically I helped him lift the stone and manoeuvre it back into position. Inch by inch it ground its way home, till there was nothing to distinguish it from its fellows.

"However did Bryn discover the cavity?" I asked.

"He played all round here when he was a boy. Used to hide things in it even then, but never told anyone about it. So when he needed a secret hiding place, it was the obvious choice."

"And – Dick Harvey?"

"God knows how he stumbled on it. Of course, the corridor

is one of the features of the castle. Being an archaeologist, I suppose he'd pay it particular attention. It's even possible that when Sinbad brought the Zimmermans he didn't push it far enough back, either, though I can't believe he'd be so careless."

"The Zimmermans came *here*?"

"Yes; Bryn wasn't happy about it because, as you said, it doubled the risk, but they flew over specially; insisted on seeing what they were paying out for. Come on, then, let's get out of here – I could do with some fresh air. Shall I go first again?"

He moved ahead of me, holding his hand out behind him. I put mine into it, and this time he held it loosely. Balance restored, I thought – or perhaps it was simply that he was more relaxed now the first part of our mission was accomplished.

We came up the final flight of steps like divers emerging from the deep, and leant for several minutes against the sun-warmed stone, blinking in the brightness. It seemed strange to be back so quickly among the crowds, when less than two minutes previously we'd been alone with our secret.

"Anything else you want to see?"

I shook my head. "Let's go."

"Right, we'll find somewhere to eat lunch."

The sun was warm on our backs as we went down the hill. Philip whistled tunelessly under his breath, but my mind was still seething with my discovery. Two million pounds' worth of paintings! Where had they come from?

Outside the cottage, the woman was still selling brochures. There was no sign of a dog – a small comfort. But as we drew near to the car park I stiffened.

"What's the matter?"

"Look!"

His eyes followed mine. Immediately alongside our car was a small red Austin.

"Good heavens, girl, there are hundreds of that model – it

doesn't have to be the same one. Anyway, you said it passed us, back on the main road."

"It did; it must have turned round and come back."

"Don't look like that, Clare; there's no need to panic."

"Oh, none at all! We're only about to remove some of the world's great art treasures, that's all. Let's shout it from the rooftops!"

"Be reasonable, now!"

"I'm not eating my lunch here," I said firmly.

"Fine, we'll find somewhere else. Get in."

He switched on the engine. "The driver's probably one of those," he said, nodding to where groups of picnickers huddled on the grass over hampers and primus stoves.

"Then the sooner we're away from them, the better." I reflected wryly that I seemed more worried than Philip did.

As we jolted over the grass, I settled back against the warm leather of my seat, slotting the latest pieces of the jigsaw into place. Elmer Zimmerman, that bald, unprepossessing man, was buying some two million pounds' worth of masterpieces from Bryn, and shipping them, presumably, to the States. But how had Bryn got hold of them in the first place, and what of Carol Lawrence, whose baby it was?

There was nothing now to stop me going to the police – nothing but the thought of what would happen to Philip. And in that moment I acknowledged two things. The first was that even if he had the Crown Jewels hidden in Cefn Fawr, I could not lift a finger to stop him, if by so doing I placed him in any kind of danger. And the second, following on that, was that I myself was his greatest potential threat, since I was the forged link in the chain.

I knew then that whatever the consequences, I had to tell him the truth, today, before he went back to the hotel to find Carol Lawrence waiting.

Chapter Eleven

'Pour out the pack of matter to mine ear,
The good and bad together.'
Shakespeare: *Antony and Cleopatra*

PHILIP was not driving fast. The high hedges slipped gently past us on either side as the road began to rise again. I barely saw them; all my attention was centred on trying to find the best way to admit how I had deceived him.

With every minute my sick apprehension grew; it was entirely possible this new, hard Philip would report me to Bryn, and there was no knowing how he would react. On the other hand, Philip might think I'd deliberately made a fool of him, and exact his own revenge. For there was no denying that almost all I had learned had been directly from him.

Over and over I practised the opening words of my confession, but none of them seemed right. For I now realised that my thoughtless dabbling in what didn't concern me was directly responsible for bringing us both into real danger.

His voice interrupted me. "Keep your eyes open for a picnic spot."

I moistened dry lips. "We must be out of sight of the road."

"Still worrying about that car? It wasn't necessarily following us, you know, just going in the same direction."

I was not reassured; at that moment the whole world seemed a threat.

When I didn't speak, he added, "He was making no attempt to keep out of sight, was he?"

"Nevertheless, he doubled back to the castle when he found he'd lost us."

"Or simply missed the turning the first time."

I shook my head. Philip hadn't believed me about Dick either, at first. "Look, there's a turning here. Let's try that."

He made a sharp turn and we found ourselves amid the branches of a little copse. The track wound on out of sight, but a short way down on the left was a five-barred gate.

Philip pulled off the lane on to the grass edging it and stopped. Getting out of the car, I was relieved to see that a large, leafy bush screened us from anyone passing on the road.

Beyond the gate lay a field, sloping away a little to the south-west, enclosed on the two nearer sides by high hedges. Over to the right and now several miles distant, Cefn Fawr raised its grim fortress to the sky, a reminder that my explanations were overdue.

Philip handed me the packed lunches. "You take these while I get the cool-bag out of the boot – I put the drink cans in it. And I'll bring my mac to sit on; the grass will be wet after yesterday."

I slipped the retaining wire off the gate and it swung open. The field was warm and sheltered and smelt of clover. We spread the mac in the right-angled corner nearest the gate and I unpacked the sandwiches and fruit, still worrying how I could tell what must be told.

Philip handed me a can of shandy and a plastic mug and gestured to the sandwiches. "Help yourself."

My heart had started a series of low, thudding beats which I thought he must surely hear. "Not for the moment."

"Aren't you hungry? I must say I am." He took a sandwich and bit appreciatively into it. The time could no longer be delayed. Carefully I set down the shandy can. It had made my hand very cold.

"Philip, there's something I have to tell you."

"Sounds serious. Can't it wait till after lunch?"

"No. If I don't tell you now, I'll never be able to. And Lord knows what would happen then." My voice shook and he raised an eyebrow.

"All right, go ahead if you must." He reached for another sandwich.

The sun was warm on my head and the stubbly grass patches felt knobbly under the macintosh. I pressed my hand down on them. My mouth was very dry.

"I'm afraid I lied to you – at least by implication. I'm not Goldilocks."

I didn't look at him. Time stretched between us, measured by my heartbeats. Then he put down the sandwich he was holding. "What are you talking about?"

"I don't know Bryn – I've never seen him in my life – and until just now at the castle, I hadn't the remotest idea what all this was about."

There was a brief, taut silence, then he said harshly, "Is this some kind of game, Clare?"

My nails bit into my palms. "No, honestly – you've got to believe me!"

"How *can* I believe you?" His voice was like a whiplash. "You know I'm Aladdin, don't you, and all about Sinbad and Beanstalk. Are you trying to tell me you're psychic or something?"

I shook my head hopelessly. "Please, Philip, just listen."

Stumblingly I began to tell him what had happened, beginning with the missed turning on the M4 and my decision to look for the hotel where he'd stayed with Matthew. And all the time I kept my eyes fixed on the ground, distractedly tearing up handfuls of grass as I spoke. But I knew, as he sat immobile, listening, that his own eyes never left me. I could feel them burning into me, trying to determine if I was, after all, telling the truth.

When I'd finished, with the letter enclosing the plan of the castle being pushed under my door, there was a long silence.

My heartbeats were drumming in my ears, pulsing in my temples. Above them, I could hear the carefree chirruping of a cricket in the long grass.

Then Philip said tonelessly, "My God!"

"I'm sorry," I said through stiff lips.

"Sorry!" He gave a harsh bark of laughter. "Good God, Clare!" His voice deepened as the full implications began to strike him. "What possessed you to let yourself get embroiled?"

I said dully, "I told you, I didn't realise it was dangerous – not until I'd seen the plan and it was too late to draw back. I – I thought it was some kind of game."

"Then how did you know about Bryn?"

"I didn't, until you told me. He'd signed himself 'Jack'."

Philip said without expression, "If they find out, they'll kill you."

"I know," I said, and shivered.

"Then why are you telling me now?"

"Because the real Goldilocks will be there when we get back."

He stared at me frowningly. "How do you know?"

"There was a note in your room – before you arrived – saying she'd been delayed. I took it." I stared fixedly at the gold disc that was the top of the shandy can.

"You bloody little fool!"

"I know, but there's no point in going into that now. What are you going to do?"

"What would *you* have done, if Aladdin had been someone else?"

"I'm not sure. I was planning to find out as much as I could, and then go to the police. At the time, though, I'd very little to go on."

"And now that I've obligingly filled you in?" His voice was dangerous.

I said, "Somehow you'll have to trust me, Philip. I swear to you that if you – if you let me go, I won't contact the police."

He said oddly, "If I let you go?"

116

I licked my lips. "I realise I've no claim on you, none whatever. But for Uncle's sake—"

I stopped and at last looked up at him. His face was pale beneath the tan, and there was an expression in his eyes that I couldn't begin to understand. He said violently, "*Clare!*" and then, a little shakily, "Do you honestly think—"

I waited, watching him anxiously, and he drew a deep breath. "How much exactly do you know? This is important."

"Well, Jack is really this man called Bryn, who seems to be the organiser. Why all these code names, anyway?"

"Because, as I said, he's obsessed with secrecy and was afraid of information falling into the wrong hands." He gave a mirthless laugh. "Ironic, that."

"You're Aladdin, of course," I hurried on, "and one of them at the hotel is Sinbad." I stopped, glanced at him and away again. "Then there's Goldilocks. You were right, by the way, it is Carol Lawrence."

Philip drew in his breath sharply.

"You said it was her 'baby', though I don't know why. Anyway, Bryn apparently hid these paintings in the castle after the fire, though *what* fire—"

I broke off. Very dimly, something was beginning to stir at the back of my memory.

"Go on," Philip ordered.

"Well, later, when the – insurance had paid up, Bryn instructed you to go to the States to find a buyer, and somehow or other you came up with the Zimmermans. They followed you back over here, outwardly on holiday but really, as you said earlier, to see what was on offer before they signed anything. And Sinbad took them to see the paintings."

"Go on," he said again.

"Well, they're to be removed from the castle on Tuesday night and taken to Swansea docks—"

"I laid that on a plate for you, didn't I?" Philip said bitterly.

"No doubt they'll be removed before they reach the US coastline."

117

"By helicopter."

"Yes. Well, that's about it. Except that you said they were worth a couple of million."

"In other words, there's precious little you don't know."

"I suppose not." I pulled nervously on a blade of grass.

"So how in God's name can I expect you not to go to the police, now that you have it all so pat? You, a respectable, law-abiding citizen!" He made it sound like an insult.

"Because I promised," I said, aware of sounding naive.

"Because you promised!" he repeated heavily. "Ye gods!"

"And because," I went on raggedly, "I don't want anything to happen to you."

"Matthew again. I've a lot to thank him for, haven't I?"

"No, not because of him this time."

My voice was barely audible, and I don't think he heard me. He was saying roughly, "And no doubt he's the reason you expect me not to give you away?"

"I know it's a lot to ask."

"One hell of a lot. For a start, how am I going to explain you? That's the immediate problem if, as you say, Carol will be there when we get back."

"I know; you'll have to switch to her, and it's bound to cause comment. The trouble is, we don't know how many of them there are at the hotel, but Sinbad at least will be suspicious, having given all the information to me."

"You can't go back," Philip said, "that's clear enough. I'll run you to the nearest station and you can make your way back to London. After that, you're on your own."

I shook my head. "It wouldn't work. For one thing, it would confirm that I know something, and they'd have no difficulty tracking me down – my address is in the register and Bryn would find me in minutes. Also, how could you explain my sudden disappearance, specially after what happened to Dick? It would look extremely suspicious."

He bent forward and put his head in his hands. "Have you any better suggestions?"

"You could tell Carol you thought I *was* Goldilocks, until I complained someone was playing tricks on me. I'd thrown the letters away, and you retrieved them from my waste-paper basket."

"Hardly convincing. Anyway, I *wouldn't* have mistaken you if I'd received her message."

"Then miss out that bit. Just say we knew each other in London. I told someone that, and at least it's the truth. Sinbad will be slated for not checking more thoroughly, but as long as everything goes off all right, perhaps it won't matter."

He said caustically, "You're forgetting that your pal Morgan witnessed our meeting, when we were playing according to the script. I can hardly go through the same routine with Carol."

He ran a hand distractedly through his hair. "I'll have to get word to her to act as though we don't know each other – which, of course, we don't – and say I'll explain later. God, what a mess. And you're really telling me you'll let those paintings leave the country without lifting a finger to stop them?"

"Yes. I swear it."

"And you still don't know where they came from?"

I stirred, staring at his half-eaten sandwich. It was curled and dry now, the once moist ham dark and hard.

"I seem to remember hearing of a fire in a gallery somewhere. They managed to save a lot of the pictures, but several valuable ones were lost."

"The word 'lost' is suitably ambiguous."

I said quickly, "I don't want to know any more."

He was staring down at the grass. "Then we come to us," he said.

I swallowed. "How do you mean?"

"Today we're all lovey-dovey on a picnic, this evening I go after someone else."

I drew a long, unsteady breath. "That's easily explained; you overstepped the mark and I gave you the brush-off."

"It has a familiar ring."

119

Anthea Fraser

Sudden tears stung my eyes. I said tartly, "Can you think of anything better?"

He didn't answer directly. "Let's recap, then. To anyone at the hotel who *isn't* involved, your charming scenario will hold good. You give me the push, so I make a play for Carol. Incidentally, how many people did you tell that you were expecting me?"

I thought back. "Only Clive and Morgan. But the waiter, Harry, knew already, even before I did. Philip, *he* must be Sinbad!"

Philip said grimly, "If any one of those three is, God help us. We'll just have to play it by ear. And what if, despite Carol's arrival, Sinbad goes on thinking you're Goldilocks?"

"We'll have to convince him otherwise."

"All right. I don't like it one bit, but since I seem to have no choice I'll play it your way. I just wish to God you were safely in London and had never set foot in this damned place."

A cloud moved over the sun and I shivered, only too aware now of the dangers that faced us. For behind those pantomime names were dangerous men, intent on the fortune almost within their grasp, and neither Philip nor I could expect any mercy from them if our deceit was uncovered.

Hard on that thought, I said urgently, "Look, you asked me earlier to drop this for Uncle's sake; now I'm asking – begging – you. *Please* don't go through with it. We can go to the police now, tell them where the paintings are, and lie low till they're recovered and everyone's rounded up. Oh, please, Philip!"

"You forget," he said drily, "that I'm as heavily involved as the rest of them. If, as you put it, 'everyone's rounded up', that'll include me."

"But if you tell the authorities—"

"Turn coppers' nark, you mean? Save my own bacon at the expense of my colleagues?"

I caught desperately at his arm, feeling him stiffen. "But suppose something goes wrong? What would happen to you?"

He tilted my head back, forcing me to meet his eyes. They

were a deep, burning blue. "It seems to me," he said softly, "that you're more concerned about my welfare now I'm a seasoned criminal, than when I was an upright insurance man. Right?"

I nodded speechlessly, and a few of the tears spilled on to my cheeks. He said something under his breath and, his hand still on my throat holding me away from him, kissed me once, bruisingly. His eyes when they met mine again were unreadable.

"That's by way of apology," he said unevenly, "for ever thinking you could be—"

He broke off and his fingers made a brief, caressing movement as they left my throat. I caught at his hand and held it tightly between mine, tears now raining down my face. I had no pride left, no control, just the need to keep him with me, and if possible out of danger.

"But there must be some way out! I couldn't bear it if anything happened to you—"

He tore his hand away, his eyes blazing in his white face.

"Stop it, Clare, just stop it – do you hear? Don't you realise how long we've been working on this thing, the planning, the timing, all the intricate details? Then you come blundering along and expect me to chuck it all in just to please you! Well, God help me, once I might have done, but not any more. As it is, you near as dammit ruined the whole operation. So for God's sake stop crying and pull yourself together. And—" his voice was low and vicious – "leave me alone!"

I gazed at him, shock drying the tears on my face, and he turned violently away and started to gather up the uneaten food. Unmoving, almost unbreathing, I watched him, the lines on his face etched as if in stone, his mouth grim.

So it had come to this. Philip now regarded me as I once had him – someone whose presence was unwelcome, to be brushed out of the way, escaped from. What satisfaction it must have given him, to see me beginning to love him, to make me admit it.

My breathing steadied to a series of deep, shuddering gasps.

121

A bird called suddenly from the hedge, and it was as if a spell had been broken. A shaft of sunlight struck the gold shandy can, hurting my throbbing eyes.

He spoke at last, and only an undercurrent in his voice gave any hint of the emotional storm that had passed between us.

"So we've established that, as far as the people at the hotel are concerned, I tried to get out of line and was dealt with accordingly. Are you going to slap my face, or do we take that as read?"

"I'm not in the mood for facetiousness," I said, with what little dignity was left to me. I got to my feet and he bent to pick up the mac and shake it out. In silence we made our way back to the car, and in silence we drove all the interminable way back to the hotel. If there had been a red car behind us, with machine guns sticking out of each window and a James Bond smokescreen behind, I doubt if either of us would have noticed it.

As we turned off the main road, I made my stiff little speech. "I should like to apologise for making an exhibition of myself. It must have been the strain. I promise you it won't happen again."

Philip's reaction took me by surprise. His foot jammed on the brake and the car rocketed to a halt. He said, "Clare – don't! I'm sorry if—"

But I'd had more than enough of his cat-and-mouse games. I wrenched open the car door and half fell out, regained my balance and started to run stumblingly down the unmade road, through the gateway and across the gravel to the hotel. I pushed my way through the swing doors and stopped short.

I could hardly have made a more effective entrance. Afternoon tea was about to be taken into the lounge. There were several people in the hall, but through the mist of my tears I registered only Harry, the waiter.

"Mr Hardy will not be sitting at my table for dinner," I said clearly. Then, aware of the staring faces, I snatched my key and ran up to my room, where I flung myself on the bed in a storm of tears.

Chapter Twelve

'. . . waste and solitary places;'
                    Shelley: *Julian and Maddalo*

BY DINNER-TIME I had, at least outwardly, regained my composure. With head high, I went downstairs and into the dining-room.

My table, sure enough, was set for one only, but Dick Harvey's next to mine was also laid. Surely – but no, I'd under-estimated Harry's tact. Philip was already seated across the room; my neighbour must be the newly arrived Goldilocks.

The interest that our separation was causing was almost palpable, and I felt the colour flame in my cheeks. But this, after all, was the impression we'd intended to convey. He hadn't looked in my direction, and after that one quick glance, I ignored him.

Morgan paused at my table. "Have a good picnic?"

"Diabolical," I said.

"Hence the segregation?"

"Please, Morgan—" I looked up, and his eyes widened as he saw my face.

"That bad?"

I said in a low voice, "Everyone's looking," and felt the gentle pressure of his hand.

"I'll see you after dinner."

He'd just seated himself when Carol came in. There was a moment of total silence, every knife and fork immobilised. I looked up, and my heart contracted. So this was what Bryn had meant by 'initial impact'.

She was the most striking girl I'd ever seen. Her hair was so pale as to be almost white, cut very short, with jagged points framing her face. Her skin was a clear, sun-ripe gold, her eyes green and thickly lashed, her mouth sensuous. There was no denying she was beautiful, but I instinctively disliked her.

She stood arrogantly just inside the room, as though acknowledging everyone's attention. Philip shouldn't find it difficult to make advances to her; the only danger would be his being trampled in the rush.

Harry hurried towards her, almost tripping in his eagerness, and ushered her to her table, which service she acknowledged with a gracious inclination of her head. Her almond eyes flicked over me without interest, then circled the room, and heads turned hastily away. All but one. Across the room, Philip's eyes met and held hers. I felt a little sick.

I made a passable attempt to eat my meal, and it ended at last. Looking neither to left nor right, I went out into the hall. Morgan followed me and took my arm. "Now, tell uncle what happened."

I moved evasively.

"Don't say it's none of my business, because I rather think it is."

I recited the line we'd agreed: "He was taking too much for granted, that's all." And added quickly, "What do you think of the new arrival?"

"A bit obvious for my taste, but Master Philip seemed impressed."

So he too had seen that exchange of looks.

"To hell with them both," he said cheerfully. "Let's see about some coffee."

Several people were already in the lounge, and Phyllis Bunting had as usual taken up her position behind the urn. We joined the Mortimers, and after a slightly hesitant start, our conversation was natural enough. No one mentioned Philip, and though, in ones and twos, the other diners came through to join us, he and Carol were not among them. They must have gone directly to the bar.

After a few minutes the groups divided and re-formed. The Zimmermans and the teachers set up a table for bridge and the Mortimers announced their intention of going for a drink.

"Are you two coming?" Pauline asked. Morgan was getting to his feet, but I shook my head.

"Not just yet."

With a surprised glance, he sat down again, and the Mortimers, with a casual, "See you later, then", left the room.

"Don't you want a drink?" Morgan inquired.

I said steadily, "If you don't mind, I'd rather not go in the bar this evening. But don't let me stop you." Brave words; I was praying he wouldn't leave me.

He looked taken aback. "There's nothing else to do."

"Couldn't we just stay here? Play bridge, or something? I think there's another card table."

"Bridge?" The look on his face was almost comical. "Good God, you're not serious?"

"I am – really. I'd much prefer to stay here." I'd no intention of watching Philip and Carol's manoeuvres.

Morgan turned resignedly to the Dacombes, who were sitting reading. "You don't play bridge, by any chance?"

Andrew looked up. "We do, as it happens. Would you like a game?"

"Oh I would, very much!" I turned to Morgan. "Please!"

He shrugged. "Very well, if you won't change your mind."

A second card table was set up, and packs of cards produced from a drawer in the sideboard. I deliberately seated myself with my back to the glass wall; Philip wouldn't have the satisfaction of my seeing him with Carol.

Across the room the other players were silent except for bidding and the slap of the cards. The old ladies sat tranquilly knitting.

Andrew fanned out the cards. I picked one, drawing a queen, and him as my partner. I started to deal.

The evening wore on, largely in silence. From time to time I glanced at the other three round the table, and wondered indifferently what they were thinking. Andrew had been looking for something in the TV room last night. Was he Sinbad? And though 'Cinderella' hadn't been mentioned, Cindy could also be involved. As for Morgan, who could guess what was going on behind that high, intelligent forehead?

The other game ended before ours, and the Zimmermans, with a nod in our direction, left the room. We finished the third rubber at exactly ten-thirty.

"Would you mind if we stopped there?" Cindy asked.

I shook my head. The game had passed the evening, which was all I'd asked of it.

"Suits me." Morgan laid down his cards with an expression of relief.

"Thanks for the game, everyone." As I stood up, easing my aching back, the sound of voices reached us. Without volition I turned, and through the glass wall saw Philip and Carol coming out of the bar. Their heads were close together and they were laughing. Philip slipped a casual arm round her and led her into the TV lounge. The door shut behind them.

I turned back to the room and to three pairs of sympathetic eyes.

Morgan said, "How about a night-cap, Clare?"

No reason, now, to avoid the bar, and I wasn't yet ready to be alone with my worries. I could hold them at bay for a few more minutes.

"Thanks, I'd like one."

In the cocktail lounge, the Zimmermans had settled themselves in a corner, and greeted us with a smile and a friendly, "Good game?"

Clive and Pauline were seated on stools, chatting to the barman about his sister's wedding.

"It was a great day," Dai finished, "but the news about Mr

126

Harvey when I got back spoilt it all. One of our regulars he was, see. I still can't believe it."

"None of us can," Clive said soberly.

Pauline, catching sight of Morgan and me, slipped off her stool. "Come and talk to me, Clare."

I followed her to a table, wondering what the Americans had made of Philip's volte-face. Morgan brought my drink and then rejoined Clive at the bar. Pauline was studying me anxiously.

"Is everything all right?" she asked in a low voice.

"Yes," I said awkwardly, "fine."

"It's none of my business, I know, but if it would help to talk—?"

My fingers tightened on my glass. "We had a row, that's all. It's no big deal."

"But Clive said you knew each other from home?"

"So?" I forced a laugh. "That doesn't necessarily ensure sweetness and light – quite the reverse!"

"I meant it wasn't just a—" She broke off, glanced at my closed face, and patted my hand. "Sorry – let's talk about something else. What have you and Morgan been doing with yourselves all evening? We expected you to join us."

"We were playing bridge."

Her eyebrows lifted. "Hidden talents! Who were you playing with?"

"The Dacombes. They won."

Mamie Zimmerman laid down her book and smiled at me. "I didn't realise you played. It's unusual these days to find young people who do, but when I was a girl, bridge was regarded as a social asset."

The fact that she'd picked up so easily on our conversation made me wonder uneasily if she'd been as interested in her book as she'd appeared. She might well have also heard my comments about Philip – not, I thought wearily, that it mattered.

"My parents taught me," I told her, "but I'm a bit rusty."

Morgan and Clive joined us at the table and conversation

became general. I was tired after the traumas of the day, and as I watched the animated faces around me, the situation seemed more and more unreal. Behind this façade of social affability, two of our number were negotiating to buy stolen art treasures, and quite possibly someone other than myself was aware of it. I wondered a little hysterically what would happen if I started to recite the ridiculous code names we'd been given.

It was obviously time I went to bed. I stood up, excused myself, and left the room, devoutly hoping I shouldn't bump into Philip and Carol in the hall. But there was only Mr Davies at the desk.

"Everything all right, Miss Laurie?" he asked as he handed me my key.

"Fine, thanks."

He grinned. "No more mysterious messages?"

I glanced nervously over my shoulder, but the hall remained empty. I forced a smile. "No."

"That's good. Good-night, then."

Alone in my room, all my fears rushed to reclaim me. *I wish to God you'd never set foot in this place*, Philip had said. Me too – oh, me too!

How could I ever face Matthew? If he knew the position I was in, he'd expect me to expose Philip and the others and recover the paintings. I knew that, but I was not as strong as my uncle, who had already publicly denounced his step-son. I supposed dully that he'd had to, for the sake of the business.

But anxiety on his behalf was only a small part of my emotions now. I wondered what Philip would do, after Wednesday. If he continued in this line of business, he was bound to be caught sooner or later.

And what of myself? God knew what risks I was running by staying under the same roof as Carol, whose role I had temporarily usurped. *Would* I be considered a risk? And if so, how would they deal with me?

Again, Philip's voice spoke in my head. *If they find out, they'll kill you.*

I caught my lip between my teeth, tasting blood, warm and salty, on my tongue. And in the meantime, what was going on in the television lounge? Was Carol satisfied with the story of the misdirected notes? There was nothing else I could do. As Philip had pointed out, I'd already done more than enough. The scalding memory of the scene in the field flooded my mind, and I covered my ears as if to shut out the cruelty in his voice.

Mechanically I undressed and crept into bed, shivering despite the comparative mildness of the night. Gradually the sounds outside my room lessened and ceased. The landing light went out and the hotel settled down to sleep. And at last I was able to force my aching eyes shut and, turning on my side, I also slept.

* * *

The next morning, I was aware of an animal-like need of privacy in which to lick my wounds, somewhere there was no chance of seeing Philip and Carol.

Accordingly I phoned down to reception and asked if there was any chance of an early breakfast. I was told there was and, spurred by my decision, had a quick bath, dressed in jeans and T-shirt, and went down to the empty dining-room. It was seven-thirty.

Outside, the wind was blowing clouds across the sky, and the room was filled with a grey, watery light. Harry brought me cereal and orange juice, a boiled egg, toast and coffee. I ate quickly, anxious to be away before any of the other guests arrived.

The room had an expectant air, with the clean stiff table-cloths and shining cutlery, the meticulously folded newspapers on each table. It was like a stage set, waiting for a play to begin. I smiled grimly to myself, wondering what Mr and Mrs Davies would make of the action going on in the wings.

"Thank you, Harry, that was good. Would you please tell Mrs Davies I shan't be in for lunch?"

129

"Very good, miss. Will you be wanting a packed lunch again?"

"No thanks, I'll stop somewhere when I'm hungry."

I had brought my jacket down to save going back upstairs. I retrieved it and was through the swing doors and across the car park before anyone else appeared.

It was the first time I'd been in my own car since my arrival – was it really only three days ago? – and I breathed a sigh of relief as I turned out of the private road on to the main one. Today was mine. I had the paperback, still unread, in my handbag, and I shouldn't have to make polite conversation to anyone. The realisation that I was free of the hotel and all it contained for at least ten hours was like a tonic.

The wind through the sunroof lifted my hair as I drove and a sudden burst of sunshine made my heart a little lighter. I resolved to close my mind to Philip and Carol and Bryn, to Morgan with his worried eyes and Clive and his easy morals, even to Andrew and Cindy, whose linked hands made my heart ache with loneliness. Today was mine alone, and I determined to enjoy it to the full.

I drove for about an hour, without any clear thought of where I was going. I followed little-used farm roads, ran through tiny grey-stone villages and alongside winding streams. Eventually, beside one such stream, I drew in the car and stopped.

Except for the soft murmuring of water, the silence was total. A steep bank led down to the brook, and beyond it, the tall, waving grasses of a meadow stretched up towards a sprawling hillside, patterned with patchwork fields on the lower slopes and rising to green woods and bare grey rock.

I picked up my book and made my way down to the water. Here, I was out of the wind. I slipped off my sandals. The bank of the little river shelved gently, with patches of soft warm sand. I sat down on one of these, and the grassy bank rising behind me was just the right height for a back rest. Above me, clouds raced across the pale sky and seabirds hung lazily in the currents of air. Here at last was the peace I had come to Wales to find.

Slowly and lazily the morning passed. Every now and then I lifted my eyes from the book to watch my toes gently burrowing in the sand, or the glint of a fish in the trickling water. I began to wish that I had after all brought a picnic lunch and need not move from this spot. By one o'clock I was really hungry, and reluctantly brushed the sand from my feet, gathered up my things, and stood up.

It was then, with a sense of shock, that I saw him – a man sitting motionless some fifty yards downstream, screened (by design?) from where I'd been sitting by a curve in the bank. Then I saw he had a line in the river; only a fisherman, after all. Or was he after bigger fish?

He didn't turn his head as I hastily made my way up the bank and back to the car.

Having passed several likely-looking pubs earlier, now that I needed one it was about ten minutes before my search was rewarded in the shape of a small flint building with deep eaves and a welcome notice outside that said *Lunches*.

They served me leek soup and apple charlotte with thick yellow cream. The men at the bar were talking Welsh among themselves. I wished fruitlessly that I had found a little place like this on Friday, instead of the more efficient but infinitely more dangerous Carreg Coed.

During lunch the pale sky deepened to a more ominous purple, and I remembered the seabirds that had flown inland. Perhaps another storm was on the way, and today I hadn't Philip's hand to hold. I wondered if he kept glancing at my empty table, or whether by now he'd joined Carol at hers.

It was only as I was leaving that I noticed the fisherman I'd seen earlier, seated in one of the alcoves with a steak pie in front of him. He must have come in after me – had he been following me? Yet this pub was the nearest to the spot where we'd spent the morning, and an obvious place for lunch.

I paused fractionally by his table, willing him to look up and meet my eye, but the sporting paper was open beside him and he appeared engrossed in it.

131

I paid my bill and went outside, thankful at least to see no sign of a red Austin in the car park.

Telling myself I was being over-imaginative, I stood for a minute to take stock of my surroundings, staring across the valley to the brooding darkness of the crags on the opposite side.

As I watched, the sun came out suddenly like liquid spilling from a jug, and its light poured over the purple peaks, staining them gold. The brightness spread rapidly down the hillside and the shadows sped before it, retreating from the white farmhouses which now twinkled like diamonds in the radiance. On it rolled across the valley floor as the clouds above parted, and in a matter of seconds I myself, in the pub doorway, stood bathed in its false warmth. Then, as suddenly, the light was withdrawn and the crags leapt back into the shadows. I shivered and turned to the car.

But although I continued my aimless meandering, my day was spoilt. The double sighting of the fisherman, innocent though no doubt he was, had unnerved me, and thick clouds now hung over the countryside with a brooding menace which my imagination was only too ready to interpret as personal. The breeze had freshened and I couldn't find another spot like my sheltered stream, where I could sit out of the car.

Still unsettled, I kept an eye on the rear-view mirror for an hour or so, and though one or two cars overtook me from time to time, there was none that seemed to be loitering behind. Finally satisfied I was not being followed, I drew off the road in the lee of a hill and took my book out again. The story reached out for me and I became absorbed, no longer noticing the changing pattern of the sky.

It was four o'clock when I next looked at my watch and belatedly realised I'd no idea where I was, nor of the way back to the hotel. My road atlas was little help on these moorland roads, and I'd no large-scale maps like Philip's.

I drove back on to the road, reversed, and turned back the way I'd come, telling myself I'd ask for directions at one of the villages I'd driven through.

But somewhere I must have taken a wrong turning, for after a while I realised I was no longer on the same road, and though I drove with increasing anxiety for mile after mile, I came across no sign of habitation, nor even any fellow motorists.

I was beginning to have visions of spending the night on the moors when, just before five, I came at last to a village, and learned from the lady in the post office that I must have been driving in a circle, and the hotel was still over an hour's drive away.

She gave me directions, and eventually, after what seemed much longer than an hour, I rejoined the valley road just short of the Plas Dinas.

Fleetingly I thought of Bronwen and Gareth, and wished it was they who'd be awaiting me instead of the sullen Mair and shifty Evan, to say nothing of Sinbad and Goldilocks. And Philip.

The fears and doubts from which I'd escaped all day came rushing back in a wave of apprehension. Reluctantly and with deepening unease, I turned off the road into the gateway of the Carreg Coed hotel.

Chapter Thirteen

'Mad, bad and dangerous to know.'

Lady Caroline Lamb: *Journal*

"CLARE! Where the *hell* have you been?"

I turned, startled, from reaching for my key, to find Morgan beside me.

"I went for a drive; why?"

"I've spent most of the day looking for you!"

I frowned. "Whatever for?"

He made an obvious attempt to control himself. "You seemed so upset last night, I was worried about your being alone. You didn't tell me you were going out."

"Why should I?" I retorted, stung by his proprietorial manner. "I'm not accountable to you for my movements."

"Clare—" He reached out and took hold of my arm. "Forgive me, I didn't mean to annoy you." He smiled a little wryly. "It's just that, now Philip's out of the running, I'd hoped we could have spent the day together."

"Well, as you can see, I'm perfectly all right," I said coolly. "Now, if you'll excuse me I must go and change or I'll be late for dinner."

And as he still hesitated, I picked up my key and went past him up the stairs.

By the time I reached my room, I'd forgotten about Morgan and his importunities and was wondering how Philip and Carol had spent their day. He'd almost certainly have taken her to the castle, to show her the layout and plan the assault. No doubt she'd have been more help to him than I was; it was her 'baby', whatever that meant.

It occurred to me that although Philip had the brochure, the notes and letters were still in my possession. Swiftly I took them out and re-read them in the light of what I now knew.

With only Sinbad's identity still outstanding, they were quite explicit enough to take to the police – which, I reminded myself, had been my original intention. Now, in view of Dick's death and its possible link with the paintings, it was even more imperative. The only question was whether I could avoid implicating Philip.

I stood in an agony of indecision, the letters in my hand. Dick was dead, I reasoned, and no amount of speedy action on my part could bring him back. Surely one more day would make no difference, and it'd give Philip a chance to get clear. There should still be time to intercept the paintings.

My conscience partly assuaged, I replaced the letters in their hiding-place and hurriedly prepared for dinner.

With the beautiful Carol very much in mind, I took out my prettiest dress, an openwork crochet in deep coral pink. It complemented my tan and helped to restore my rocky self-confidence.

In fact, its effect became apparent only too soon, for as I closed my bedroom door behind me, a pair of arms came round me from behind and a voice said in my ear, "How do you always manage to look so delectable?"

I struggled round in the circle of arms to see Clive Mortimer smiling down at me. And in the second that we stood there, our faces close and his arms still round me, Philip's door opened and shut. I pulled myself free and turned quickly to face him. His eyes were completely expressionless.

"Good evening," he said stiffly, and walked down the corridor to the stairs.

"*Faux pas* the second!" Clive said, with a laugh in his voice.

"Isn't it time you grew up?" I demanded hotly. "Why can't you leave me alone?"

"Honey-child, if you want me to leave you alone, you should change your dressmaker." He smiled and poked one finger through the crochet-work to touch the flesh above my breast.

"I'm not one of your chambermaids!" I snapped.

"Oh-ho! Do I detect jealousy?"

Before I was aware of it, my hand had lashed out across his face – just as Pauline appeared behind him.

Cheeks flaming, I turned and fled for the stairs. As I reached the hall Morgan's voice called, "Hey, wait a minute! Whatever's wrong?"

"Everything!" I answered shakily, already ashamed of my outburst. After all, Clive was Clive. He'd meant no harm, and none would have been done had Philip not come out of his room when he did. It was, as I well knew, because he'd seen us together that I'd reacted as I did.

I made no demur as Morgan led me firmly to the cocktail lounge. Standing at the bar, still breathing fast, I caught unwelcome sight of my reflection, face the same colour as my dress and eyes stormy.

But the drink steadied me, as he'd intended. "Now," he said gently as, minutes later, I put down the glass, "we're going in to dinner, and since you seem in need of moral support, I'll sit at your table, if I may."

"Thank you," I said meekly.

During the first course he talked lightly – about the food, the weather, an amusing remark by young Stuart Mortimer – and gradually I began to relax, closing my mind to Carol, utterly ravishing in a dress of peacock-blue, laughing over her glass at Philip.

But not before Morgan had caught the direction of my glance. "I admit to being slightly puzzled—" he began, but I shook my head violently and he did not go on.

"Tell me about yourself," I said quickly, to distract him.

He smiled. "What do you want to know?"

"Well, where you live, and if you write full-time, and why nineteenth-century Welsh politics."

"Enough to be going on with! To answer in order, I live in Cardiff – by myself, if you're interested; I was divorced three years ago. And no, my books unfortunately don't make enough money for me to live on. I have a 'day job' with a local publishing firm."

"That should be useful!"

He grimaced. "Except that they don't do biographies."

"So what started you on this book?"

"I read an article about Thomas a few years ago. He'd been a fairly prominent figure locally, but little was known about his background before his rise to power. My curiosity was aroused and I began to dig."

As I'd hoped, once launched into his subject he talked for some time, about the man's charisma and gift of oratory, and about coal miners and dockers and the Industrial Revolution. At any other time I'd have been interested, but there was too much on my mind and my thoughts began to wander.

What interpretation had Pauline placed on that little scene on the landing? I should have to apologise to them both, and the knowledge did little to help my appetite.

"You're very lucky," I said, as Morgan finally came to a halt. "I wish I had a hobby that engrossed me like that. It must be so satisfying."

"It is, especially when I come across something unexpected – the draft for a famous speech, or an illegitimate child no one knew about."

There was a rattle of rain against the windows, and Harry moved to put the lights on. Immediately the garden outside sank into obscurity.

"Pity," Morgan said reflectively. "I hoped we'd seen the last of the rain."

"At least it waited till the evening."

He smiled, and something in the smile sent an unexpected tingle up my spine. I shook myself impatiently. This was

Morgan, who had comforted me, worried about me, even played bridge with me; who, in fact, had been my anchor over the last few days, a much-needed support during the chaotic confrontations with Philip.

He finished the last of his wine and put down the glass.

"Ready, Clare?"

I was watching Philip and Carol leave the room, his hand under her elbow.

"Yes, I think so."

"Let's go, then."

When we reached the hall, Carol had disappeared and Philip was standing alone, hands in pockets, staring through the swing doors at the curtain of rain. To my surprise, Morgan led me over to him. He turned quickly as we approached, and his face shuttered.

"Could you spare a minute, Philip?" Morgan spoke pleasantly. "Clare and I would like a word with you upstairs."

I shrugged free of him, flushing with furious embarrassment. "Morgan, whatever are you doing? You know I don't want—"

"Or," he went on inexorably, "if you'd like me to continue the charade, *Fee-fi-fo-fum, I smell the blood of an Englishman.*"

My breath clogged in my throat. The fact that I'd been waiting for something like this for three days did not lessen the shock when it actually came. For, though I'd certainly considered him in the role, this was the man who, only two minutes earlier, had been my attentive, admiring dinner partner. No wonder, I thought bleakly, he was in such a panic when I disappeared all day.

Philip had recovered more quickly. He said, "I'll come, of course, but don't involve Clare; there's been—"

"What do you mean, don't involve Clare? Don't think you can exclude her because of some stupid quarrel."

I said breathlessly, "Morgan, what is it? What's going on?"

He turned to me, and for the first time it struck me that

138

his eyes were like a snake's, hooded, glittering, dangerous. "You can stop acting now, my dear, we've finished with all the subterfuge."

"For God's sake listen to me, Rees!" Philip broke in harshly. "You're making a dangerous mistake. I can explain, but—" He turned to me. "If you wouldn't mind waiting in—?"

"Look, I've had enough of this," Morgan interrupted. "She knows everything; damn it, I gave her the information myself. Now upstairs at once, both of you."

I made one last, hopeless attempt. "What information? What are you talking about?"

With an impatient exclamation he took my arm and marched me across the hall and up the stairs. When we reached the top, I looked frantically for Carol, who might yet come to my rescue. But no one was in sight and Morgan's hand was firm on my arm.

"In we go," he said pleasantly, opening the door beyond mine. Philip followed us in. The window was open and the net curtain, caught by the wind, streamed out into the darkness like a banner. The door slammed in the sudden draught and I shivered.

Morgan pulled the net inside, shut the window, and drew across the heavy blue curtains.

"Now," he said conversationally, "there's been a change of plan. The castle is to be stormed tonight."

"Rees, in the name of heaven listen to me! You're wrong about Clare! Let her go, before she hears too much!"

Morgan spun round, his temper at last flaring. "What the hell's got into you? Let me spell it out: I passed her the notes – as instructed. You greeted her as a close friend – as instructed. I was there, remember. You took her to the castle – as instructed. What happened then, I neither know nor care. Nor do I understand the importance you're attaching to this quarrel, considering your affair's only camouflage."

He looked from one of us to the other. "I was tempted to remind you of that when I saw you both in the TV room. Surely

Bryn made it clear, as he did to me, that this girl is strictly out of bounds."

"It's nothing to do with any quarrel," Philip said in a low, urgent voice. "I can explain if you'll only let me, but first, get Clare out of here. Don't you see, man, Carol's the one you want!"

Morgan swung towards him. "Carol?" he said sharply. "The girl downstairs?"

Philip nodded. "All these bloody code names; no wonder there's been such a muddle." He drew a deep breath. "Another complication was that I knew Clare in London. It was a pure fluke, her turning up out of the blue, but it certainly compounded the mix-up."

Morgan stared from him to me, doubt and the seriousness of his error dawning in his eyes.

"I don't know what this is about," I repeated doggedly, "and I don't think I want to, so please may I go?"

Before he could reply, there was a sharp tap on the door. We all froze, staring at each other. The knock came again, more urgently. Morgan moved to the door and pulled it open. Carol Lawrence stood outside.

"Greetings, Sinbad," she said. "I've come to tell you you have the wrong Principal Girl."

I had one moment's grace, while Morgan and Carol stood facing each other, and instinctively I took it. I darted past them through the door, and heard Morgan say, "Get her!"

Carol's fingertips brushed my arm, but I hurtled past her. One of the doors opposite was half-open. Like a fox down a hole, I flung myself into the gap and slammed it behind me, my fumbling fingers pulling down the catch. Then, as a hammering started on the door and the knob rattled violently, I turned, trembling, to see Miss Hettie staring at me across the room. I faced her, my hands spreadeagled on the door behind me.

"Please – please let me stay!" I pleaded. "I don't know why, but they're after me!"

She came towards me, her bright eyes intent on my face. Her

pursed little mouth made gentle, clucking sounds of sympathy, and her face beneath the pale powder was soft and wrinkled like white velvet. She smelled of lavender.

"Poor child," she murmured softly, and moved me gently away from the door. I half leant against her, my breath tearing at my lungs, and almost in slow motion saw her hand move out to the lock. Before I could adjust to what was happening, the door was open and Morgan stood facing me.

"Thanks, Miss Olwen," he said briefly.

My disbelieving eyes slid to the little old face, smiling at me reproachfully. "We must all do as Bryn asks, Carol dear," she said. Then, to Morgan, "It's Hettie, dear – the younger one."

He took my arm, his fingers pinching my flesh, and marched me back to his room, where Philip and Carol stood waiting in silence. The door closed once more behind us and this time I knew there'd be no escape.

"They're Bryn's aunts," Carol said shortly, seeing my incomprehension. *Carol dear* – one of them had called me that my first evening.

Morgan said, "What the hell do we do now? Whatever you say, she *must* know what's happening – I gave her the plan, for God's sake. How could she not know?"

"She told Philip about it," Carol put in, perching on the dressing-table. "She thought someone was playing tricks, and consigned everything to the bin. That's where Philip found the brochure."

In his frustration, Morgan turned on her. "And what in the name of God happened to you?"

"I was in a car crash and carted off to hospital; they kept me in for two nights. My mobile was switched off, so when Bryn couldn't reach me, he tried phoning the Plas Dinas. That seems to be where the confusion started.

"But I sent a message to Philip, and naturally thought he'd pass it on to you. When he told me last night he didn't know who 'Sinbad' was, I couldn't *believe* it! It's all Bryn's fault – he's like a kid with his bloody code names."

141

"But why didn't you *tell* me?" Morgan demanded furiously.

"What chance have we had? We were going to, first thing this morning, but there was no sign of you and we couldn't hang around – we had to set off for the castle. Our next opportunity was now, after dinner, but you beat us to it."

Morgan said reflectively, "So that's why he dropped Clare when you came on the scene. But what in heaven's name do we do with her now?"

They were talking about me as though I wasn't there, but it seemed wisest not to protest. My safest course was to keep as quiet as I could and appear to offer no threat.

"Never mind her," Carol said impatiently, "we'll think of something. What I want to know is, why this unscheduled meeting?"

"Bryn's deviousness again," Morgan answered heavily. "On the principle of trusting no one, everything's been brought forward a day. Beanstalk takes place tonight, and the orders are that from the moment I tell you, we all stay together."

Behind the curtain the window shook in a frenzy of wind and rain.

"Quite a night for it!" Carol said. "Thank God I've at least seen the castle by daylight."

"But what do we do about Clare?" Morgan demanded again.

"Leave her here for now," Carol said carelessly. "Bryn'll think of something."

"But she'd have the entire Welsh police force on to us!"

"Obviously she'd have to be tied and gagged."

"No way!" Philip spoke violently. "It wasn't her fault we embroiled her in all this. Personally," he added more calmly, "I don't see why either of the girls need go. We both know the layout, Morgan; why can't we do it?"

Morgan shook his head. "Bryn was against that all along, hence the man/girl set up; if two men were spotted out in the dark, it would arouse suspicion. But we'll have to get Clare out of here; even if she was gagged, she could attract attention."

"But I wouldn't!" I interrupted, galvanised into speech. "I swear I wouldn't! Philip's father is my uncle – I wouldn't do anything to hurt him."

Morgan said shortly, "Sorry, can't risk it." He turned back to the others. "We'll have to revise our plans; originally, as you know, I was to stay here, but as things stand our best course is just to double up – two couples instead of one. Clare and I'll come with you."

He paused, but although both Philip and Carol looked uneasy, neither of them protested further, or suggested an alternative. Morgan looked at his watch. "It's nine now, and completely dark. You girls go and change into something more suitable, then come back here. Carol, stay with her all the time."

He nodded his dismissal and Carol pushed me out of the door on to the landing.

"I haven't got my key," I said. "I'll have to go down for it."

"I'll come with you."

In silence and side by side, we went downstairs. In the lounge I could see the school-teachers and the Mortimers drinking coffee. I still hadn't had the chance to apologise.

"What number is it?" Carol asked.

I told her and she reached over, took down the key, and accompanied me back upstairs. Thank heaven I hadn't left the letters out, I thought fervently, as I opened my door.

Her cool eyes watched me impersonally as I exchanged my dress for jeans and my warmest sweater. Finally I put on walking shoes, took the waterproof jacket from the wardrobe and turned to face her.

"Ready," I said, with as much lightness as I could muster.

She examined the hood on the jacket and nodded, satisfied. "You'll need that to cover your hair; it'll show up in the dark. Right, my turn."

Silently I went with her past the stairhead to the room which had been Dick Harvey's. There, having swiftly changed into a black sweater, trousers and anorak, she looked lovelier than

143

ever, face and hair glowing radiantly and her eyes alight with excitement. Tonight was the culmination of months of planning and risk-taking, and if I did anything to hinder her, she would, I knew, be totally ruthless.

Morgan and Philip must have been been listening for our return, and came out as we approached the door.

"Turn left, and through the door at the end," Morgan directed in a low voice. "It leads to the service stairs."

As we passed the Mortimer children's room, I could hear Emma murmuring in her sleep. Then we were on the back staircase. From below came the sound of voices and a sudden laugh.

Philip's voice said in my ear, "Steady!" He gripped my hand, and I felt something scrape against my palm – something small and brittle, with sharp edges. A ball of paper. My fingers closed on it, and in the same moment I saw two doors immediately opposite the foot of the stairs – the staff lavatories.

"Shan't be a minute," I said quickly, and shot inside the ladies'. I heard Morgan swear, and Carol say placatingly, "She hasn't got a mobile – I checked."

Tremblingly I unwrapped the hard little paper ball. Scribbled on it were the words: *Make a run for it and phone police. They won't waste time looking for you. Good luck!*

Philip *wanted* me to contact the police?

There was a soft, impatient knock at the door and I hastily flushed the paper away. He didn't look at me when I emerged. Morgan took my arm and hurried me out of the back door into the wind-tossed garden and round the corner of the house to the car park. The full force of the wind ripped at my jacket and I pulled it close, walking blindly, head down, through the spattering rain.

"Into the front," Morgan ordered, opening his car door. "And you in the back, Carol. Philip, get the crate for the pictures, will you? My boot is open."

We waited in silence while the transfer was completed, Morgan standing guard outside my door.

My brain had slipped into over-drive as I turned it to planning my escape. Even if he moved away, it was useless to attempt a break here. They were still very much on their guard, and after my shock with the old ladies, I wasn't sure even of the Davieses. It would have to be when we reached the castle. Somehow, I'd have to hide till they gave up looking for me and started up the hill, then knock at the cottage for help.

The two men got in the car and we were off, driving in silence through the wet, windy darkness. Again and again, I went through the scene in Morgan's bedroom, in case there was anything I'd overlooked. *On the principle of trusting no one*, he had said.

But perhaps, I thought suddenly, it was Philip Bryn was unsure of? Perhaps he *had* tipped the police to stand by tomorrow? Tonight, though, there'd be no one to stop them.

I didn't attempt to work out the details, just accepted, thankfully, that Philip and I were somehow at last on the same side, and that he had appealed for my help. It was up to me not to let him down.

With my back rigid and my eyes on the rhythmic wipers, I sat immobile as the car sped through the night, taking us ever nearer to Cefn Fawr Castle.

Chapter Fourteen

'Thou sure and firm-set earth,
Hear not my steps, which way they walk, for fear
The very stones prate of my whereabout . . .'
                    Shakespeare: *Macbeth*

IT WAS not a night one would choose to be out in. Philip and
Carol sat silently behind me; beside me, Morgan's hands were
confident on the wheel.

"Did you see old Gwilym up at the castle?" he asked
suddenly.

"If it was he who gave us the tickets," Philip answered.

"It would have been. He won't be a problem – he lives a
couple of miles away. It's the people in the cottage we have
to watch out for, and they're not likely to be about on a night
like this."

"Have they any connection with the castle?" Carol asked.

"A franchise to sell postcards, but nothing more."

I was only half listening. I'd just realised I had no money
with me. I shouldn't need it for a 999 call, but I'd no idea how
I'd find my way back to the hotel.

Click, clack, click, clack. The windscreen wipers moved
rhymically and my eyes followed them. Beyond their reach, the
blinding raindrops streamed down the glass and a little wall of
water built up on the edge of the arc, creeping forward as the
wipers swung away, pushed back on the return sweep.

I wished that Philip was making the run with me, but they

didn't know yet where his loyalties lay and of course he must stay near the paintings.

On and on the car scuttled, a small black beetle in the vastness of the night. Already the journey seemed endless, as though we were doomed for eternity to climb laboriously up one hill after another until the end of time, the whole world confined in the golden glow of our headlights. Every now and then we sped through the villages where, yesterday, Philip and I had seen children and puppies playing in the dust. Yesterday, in the sunshine, safe with Philip.

My mouth and throat were parched, painful when I tried to swallow. A little pulse jerked distractingly in my cheek and my hands, clenched on my lap, were sticky with sweat.

Carol spoke suddenly from the back seat, making me jump.

"I'm a bit nervous about the aunts, Morgan. Bryn often spoke of them, but I didn't realise they were so old; can they be trusted not to let something slip?"

"Don't worry, they're not told any details, they just supply information. His ears and eyes, Bryn calls them. They're invaluable – they look so innocent, yet they don't miss a thing.

"Personally," he added, "I'm more concerned about Harry; I had to grease his palm to pinch Mair's key and leave the note in Clare's room. I fed him some cock-and-bull story at the time – I just hope he swallowed it."

"And Evan?" I asked. "How much does he know?"

Morgan glanced at me in surprise. It was the first time I'd spoken since leaving the hotel.

"Nothing, that I'm aware of, unless Harry said something. Why?"

"I found him in my room."

He shrugged dismissively. "Looking for something to pinch, I don't doubt."

Carol said, "So what about our final briefing?"

"The original plan still holds good: you and Philip retrieve the pictures. The only difference is that Clare and I will be keeping a look-out at the foot of the hill. It should be easy to stay out of sight in this weather."

I devoutly hoped he was right.

"And if anyone does come along," he added, "they'd only take us for a courting couple."

They wouldn't waste time looking for me, Philip had said. But he was wrong: Morgan would have ample opportunity to search. For the first time, I faced the fact that I mightn't be able to escape. If I knew where the car would be left I could form some kind of plan, but I dared not ask. Oh God, I prayed desperately, let me get away! Let it be all right!

Carol lit a cigarette. The match flared in the confined space, lighting the outline of Morgan's jaw like a turnip-head on Hallowe'en. The sulphur filled my nostrils, titillating them. I wanted to sneeze, but it dried up in the desert of my mouth.

"Not much farther," Morgan said after a while. His voice had a jerky, breathless quality, as though anticipation was already quickening his heartbeat. The painful thumping of my own heart threatened to crack my ribs. I was hot in the thick sweater and jacket, but my legs and feet, despite the jeans, were icy, as though I was in the grip of fever. I hoped uneasily that they wouldn't blame Philip for my escape.

We turned on to the road leading to the castle, and Morgan asked, "Where did you decide to leave the car?"

At last! I tensed, waiting for Philip's reply.

"It was quite tricky." I could hear the strain in his voice. "The official park's too far away, but round the far side there's a track that extends for about twenty feet before ending in solid rock. You'll need to take care, though, because it's very narrow and there's only about six feet between the rock face on one side and the edge of the cliff on the other. It looked bad enough in daylight.

"As for getting up to the castle, we'll have no option but to use the public footpath – quite simply, there's no other way. We did a thorough recce this morning, without any joy."

"But the car'll be out of sight round the sea side?"

"That's right."

Difficult, I thought. A dead end, which meant I'd have to double back in the direction they'd all be taking. But when Philip had picked the spot, he hadn't known I'd be with them.

"And now, ladies and gentleman" – Morgan's voice rang with excitement – "on your left, even if you can scarcely see it, Cefn Fawr Castle!"

My nails ripped into my palms. Now, I thought, now!

Philip leant forward between us, ready to give directions. We passed the car park, barely discernible through the rain-lashed window, and came to the bumpy grass of the footpath. Ahead of us, swimming through the streaming windscreen, I could see the lights of the cottage windows. What, I wondered, if its occupants happened to look out just now?

Then, in a series of jerks, we were past and approaching the point at which the path up to the castle began to rise steeply.

"Here!" Philip instructed. "Turn left and follow the hill round."

The car obediently veered off the track, careening wildly over the uneven ground before slowing to take the corner and creeping cautiously forward as close as possible to the rock on our right.

"Anywhere here," Philip said, "but watch your tyres. Some of the loose stones are very sharp and the last thing we want is a puncture."

Morgan lurched to a stop and switched off his lights. Total darkness swooped down on us and we tacitly waited for our eyes to adjust. Rain continued to lash the windows, now impenetrable with the wipers switched off, and close at hand the sea pounded against the cliffs.

"Thank God the rolls are wrapped in polythene," Carol said. "I only wish I was!"

Morgan swivelled in his seat to face her. "Now, you both know what you have to do. All the rolls at one go – two journeys are out of the question. Then back down here, like bats out of hell. Just dump the rolls in the boot – we'll stop to pack

149

them when we're well clear. And remember, the boat leaves at midnight – there's no time to waste. Any questions?"

There was silence except for our quick breathing.

"Right, then, off you go. And good luck!"

Carol pulled the hood of her anorak over her shining hair, and I did likewise. Then we were all out of the car, gasping as the wind stole our breath. Philip, who, like me, was on the side nearest the sea, caught my hand in a fleeting pressure and moved round the car to join the others.

Bent double, I took off, running as if my life depended on it – which it might well have done. Wind and sea roared in my ears, drowning any sounds of pursuit. Had they missed me yet? The ground was treacherous and my rubber-soled shoes slithered and slipped, dislodging little stones which rattled deafeningly in my ears.

Behind me I heard a muffled shout, a low call, then running footsteps. With the breath tearing at my lungs and rain stinging my face, I ran gaspingly, stumblingly, away from them.

Their obvious course would be for Philip and Carol to go up to the castle while Morgan hung around the cottage in case I tried to get help.

Thank God my brain was still working! I paused momentarily, swallowing lungfuls of wild stormy air, for I had indeed been heading for the cottage. But the only other prospect of help was the main road – and that was some distance away.

My hair whipped out from the hood, stinging my eyes, and already there was a burning stitch in my side. What chance of finding a call box in this desolate wilderness? Yet I must contact the police – Philip was depending on me.

I stopped again, ears straining through the elements for sounds of pursuit. There were none. Perhaps Morgan had circled in front of me; perhaps he was waiting in that darker patch of shadow just ahead. The breath twisted in my throat but I forced myself on. If I started thinking along those lines, I'd be too panic-stricken to move and then he would surely catch me.

What was certain was that I must give the cottage a wide berth, which meant wasting precious time. Blindly swerving out in a semicircle, unable to see the ground under my feet, I fastened my mind on the road, now several hundred yards ahead and to the right of me. It was essential to reach it before Morgan thought to head me off there.

Had he a torch? If so, would he dare use it? I had a vision of myself running down a long tunnel of light, while Morgan came after me at his leisure. My legs went weak at the thought.

I dismissed it and, like a long-distance runner, settled down to pace myself, finding it easier to run with my mouth slightly open, allowing the cool draughts of night air to provide much-needed oxygen. The sound of my ragged breathing was loud above the wind. Once, my foot slipped into a rabbit hole and I stumbled, wrenching my ankle, but after a snatched second to rub it, went on again.

Where was Morgan now? Was he waiting for me near the cottage, and if so, might he catch a glimpse of me? By now, I was parallel with the car park. Behind me and slightly to my right, Cefn Fawr was a dark mass against a slightly lighter sky. To the left were the slopes where Philip and I had had our painful discussion. *I always knew you didn't give a damn for me . . . I loved you enough for both of us.*

Tears mingled with the rain on my cheeks and my gasping choked into a sob. If I cried now, I told myself furiously, I wouldn't be able to breathe at all.

On and on, heart pumping, muscles screaming with strain. What was happening up the hill? Had Carol and Philip reached the castle? Would they be able to get inside? I imagined Philip toppling in slow motion over the walls into the boiling sea. Or Carol stumbling down the steps in the corridor, and his catching and holding her as he'd held me.

I had reached the road, and blessedly there was no sign of Morgan. Without a pause I came off the grass on to the more even surface, and ten gruelling minutes later reached the junction where we'd turned off.

I stopped there because I had to, gulping down air and pressing my hands to my burning sides. My heart was racing thunderously, echoed by the pulse in my cheek and the roaring blood in my ears, and it seemed an iron band was pressing against my temples.

And what, I thought for the first time, do I do now? This wasn't exactly Piccadilly; in all probability, no one would come along here before morning. A phone-box or filling station, then? Possibly, but I'd no idea in which direction.

I started to jog again, following the twists and turns of the road. I'd not been along this portion of it, and tried to remember the contours of the map I'd looked at with Philip. *We rejoin this road*, he had said, *and follow it for ten miles or so.*

Ten miles! I staggered to a halt, the ready tears welling again. With my plans only half-formed, I'd been hoping to stop a car on the busier B road leading to the motorway. But it was still ten miles away! To my shaking legs and bursting lungs, it might as well have been a hundred. I glanced uncertainly behind me. Perhaps I should . . .

My heart seemed suddenly to explode, then started racing twice as fast. Because behind me, in the distance, I saw some lights. Did they belong to a house – a house with a telephone?

No, I realised a minute later, they were moving. A car, then. I dismissed a quick flash of fear; not Morgan – there hadn't been time to bring the pictures down.

The lights had vanished again, hidden by one of the many bends in the road. Suppose the car turned off somewhere before it reached me? I started to run back like a wounded hare, weaving from side to side, my ribs on fire.

Oh please, I prayed, my eyes following the fitful flashes which signalled its progress, please come this way! It couldn't be far away now. Suppose, all in black as I was, the driver didn't see me on the edge of the road? And there mightn't be another car tonight – except Morgan's.

In a frenzy of panic I tore down my hood, shaking my hair free to give extra visibility, and ran straight out on to the road as the car rounded the last curve barely twenty yards away. I was caught, pinned in the headlamps like a trapped moth. I flung my arms up over my head, bent my knees, and blindly awaited the crash of impact.

Brakes screeched, tyres seared along the wet road. The car swerved to the side and stopped on my right, with about three feet to spare. Almost as it rocked to a halt, the door crashed open and a man's voice, unsteady with shock, demanded furiously,

"What the bloody hell do you think you're doing?"

Still marvelling that I was alive, I felt myself caught roughly by the arms and pulled upright. But my legs were no longer capable of support and I promptly sagged again.

"Are you hurt?" The fury died out of the man's voice. "I didn't touch you, did I? What happened?" Strong arms lifted me as if I were a child and I was carried back to the car and gently set down in the passenger seat.

"Great heavens, girl, you look all in! What on earth are you doing in this deserted place on a night like this?"

I struggled to control my voice. "Please – will you – take me to – the nearest phone-box – or police station?"

He looked down at me frowningly. "Did someone attack you?"

I shook my head. "I just – ran away. *Please!*"

He considered for a moment. Then he said briskly, "All right. You're the boss." He slammed the door, went round to the driver's side and got in next to me.

I leant back against the leather, luxuriating in being still, letting the pounding of my heart gradually lessen. "Please – hurry!"

He switched on the ignition. "I hope you appreciate that you've knocked at least ten years off my life!"

"I'm sorry." I closed my eyes. "I was so afraid you wouldn't see me."

"You can thank God I did – and in time."

"I do," I said sincerely.

153

"But where did you spring from? Surely there's nothing within miles except a ruined castle?"

"No."

"Well?" he prompted, when I did not go on. "Where have you been and what happened to you?"

I shook my head. "I'm sorry, it's a long story and I haven't any breath to spare. Do you know if there's a phone-box along here?"

"There could be; failing that, there are the motorway services. Where are you aiming for?"

"Just the nearest phone." I couldn't think beyond that.

"When you'll miraculously have recovered enough to speak?"

"I'm sorry," I said contritely. He had, after all, come to my rescue, and been given quite a fright into the bargain. He deserved an explanation.

"It's an involved story and I don't really expect you to believe it, but the gist of it is that some priceless works of art are hidden in that castle. They're being removed tonight and taken to Swansea, from where they'll be shipped out of the country."

"And 007 entrusted you with the vital task of getting reinforcements?"

I said tiredly, "I said you wouldn't believe me."

"Ah," he said quietly, "but you see, I do. I believe every word."

Slowly my eyes opened. I turned my head to look at him, registering for the first time how good-looking he was. "You do?"

"Certainly; I grew up hereabouts and know all the traditional hiding-places."

"I don't know if it's traditional," I said doubtfully. Then I sat quickly forward. "Look – isn't that a phone-box? Oh, thank God!" I looked at him quickly. He was smiling, his eyes on the road ahead.

"There's a phone-box!" I repeated, my voice rising in

agitation. "Stop! Oh please, please!" I caught recklessly at his arm, but it might have been made of steel. The speed of the car didn't slacken. In a moment the little cube of light was lost in the darkness behind us.

I was close to tears. "Why did you do that? Where are we going?"

"I haven't decided yet," he said.

Too late, I remembered all I had read about girls who accepted lifts from strangers on lonely roads at night. I was a fool, a criminally stupid fool! My head had been so stuffed full of buried treasure and Philip's dependence on me that I'd ignored the most basic warnings that had been drummed into me from childhood.

Anger at myself steadied me a little. I asked bitingly, "Do you make a habit of this?"

"Only when a girl hurls herself under my wheels. And even then, only when she proves a nuisance."

"A nuisance?"

"Didn't it occur to you, my pretty one, to wonder why I was on this road myself at this particular time of night?"

I said slowly, "It's a main road."

"True. And to prove your point, there's another car behind us."

I spun round. Twin gold stars shimmered among the raindrops on the back window. Morgan already! I was too late!

"We've got to stop them!" I cried urgently.

He laughed. "Calm yourself; it's not your precious getaway car, but whoever it is, we'll soon lose them." And his foot went down on the accelerator.

In the wing mirror, I saw the lights dwindle into the distance. "How do you know it's not them?" I asked uneasily.

Then, all at once, I knew. And I also knew why he had so providently happened to come along. I stared at him, my eyes widening in panic.

"Sit back, there's a good girl," said Bryn genially, "and I'll tell you the whole story. We've plenty of time."

Chapter Fifteen

'Matrimonial devotion
Doesn't seem to suit her notion . . .'
                    Gilbert: *The Mikado*

IF THEY find out, they'll kill you. Well, they had found out;
it wasn't likely I'd be able to fool Bryn. As though reading
my thoughts, he said conversationally, "You're Clare Laurie,
aren't you?"

There was no point in denying it. "How do you know?"

"Carol phoned last night – I'd collected her from hospital
and we drove up together. I hadn't planned to come, but her
car was out of action and in any case she wasn't fit to drive;
they'd wanted to keep her in another day."

I felt him glance at me.

"But I was aware of you, if not your name, before that –
since Friday, in fact, when I phoned Plas Dinas to speak to
her, and was told she'd already left. I did wonder, later, who'd
received my message, but I certainly never dreamed Morgan
would think you were Goldilocks.

"I suppose, in true cloak-and-dagger fashion, I should have
provided passwords, but it hadn't seemed necessary. Carol
and Philip should have met at the Plas Dinas – where they
could hardly have mistaken each other – and when they
arrived together at Carreg Coed, it would have been clear
who they were."

The lights of a car coming towards us blossomed through

the rain. I wondered, without hope, if I could do anything to attract their attention, but they passed with a swoosh and we were alone again in the rain-filled darkness. Bryn continued:

"But as soon as she arrived, it was clear something was wrong. First there was a note from Philip, telling her to act as though they didn't know each other, instead of as lovers as arranged. Then, later," (in the television lounge, I thought) "he spun her some story about you receiving my letter and the brochure, and simply throwing them away.

"Well, you must admit that took a bit of swallowing – only natural for you to have shown *some* curiosity. So we guessed you'd found out too much, and because he knew you, he was trying to protect you."

My worst fears were realised; by trying to save me, Philip had become suspect, and unless I could get help in the next few minutes, he'd have to take them all on single-handed.

"Morgan had obviously loused it up," Bryn went on, "and Carol was set to tell him so at the first opportunity. But since you're here, as large as life, it seems she didn't get the chance."

"Not until this evening," I said.

"Ah. Well, we still weren't done with misunderstandings, because when I phoned to tell him this was D-Day, I asked if he'd sorted out 'Goldilocks', and he said yes, but she'd been out all day. I thought he meant with Philip at the castle."

"So why are you here?" I asked accusingly. "I thought you were supposed to keep out of it?"

"Well, my lovely, there've been enough hitches to make me decidedly edgy; I needed to satisfy myself that all was going well. Lucky I did, wouldn't you say?"

I doubt if he expected a reply. Surreptitiously I glanced in the wing mirror. The gold star-lights had dwindled in the distance, but they were still there, and since Bryn was trying to shake them off, they might well be a source of help.

"So what happened this evening?" he inquired with interest.

157

"Morgan took Philip and me to his room. Philip tried to say I didn't know anything, but he wouldn't believe him. Then Carol arrived." I paused. "You know, Philip did honestly think I was Goldilocks at first."

Bryn gave a snort of laughter. "Come on, Clare, you don't seriously expect me to believe that! Not when he knew you from home."

"But it was three months since I'd seen him. Anything could have happened in that time, and I had all the code names pat."

"I knew it! So much for Little Miss Innocence! Even so, I'd told him I was sending Carol."

"No, what you said was 'one of your girls'."

"Did I now? And you come into that category?"

"Philip thought so."

He glanced at me briefly. "You're in love with him, aren't you?"

I nodded.

"Then how come you haven't seen him for three months?"

I didn't reply.

"Ah, wait a minute, now. Three months – that would be the time he left the family business. Shock-horror all round. Ordered out of the house and – that's right – his engagement broken off. By you, I presume?" He shook his head in mock sorrow. "Total rejection all round – I must say I felt for him. Reckoned he could use a friendly face, so I made contact. We'd got on well before, and it seemed the least I could do."

That surprised me. "You already knew each other?" I'd assumed Philip's connections with Bryn dated from after his fall from grace.

"Yes, we met a year or two ago, when he was on holiday here. Our stays overlapped at the Plas Dinas, and we spent a couple of days fishing together."

Another car was rushing towards us, then it was past and vanishing in the distance. It struck me uneasily that we should have reached the motorway by now. Perhaps Bryn was avoiding it.

"We talked about our jobs, as you do," he was continuing, "and I thought at the time that his contacts would have been useful. But that was as far as it got, because at that stage our Philip was an upright citizen, an insurance broker no less." His voice was heavy with sarcasm.

"Still, even the mighty can fall. So when the news broke – shady dealings, dishonest handling, the lot – I got in touch, not, I admit, altogether altruistically, and offered him a job. And as I'd hoped, it paid off." His voice dropped to scarcely above a whisper. "Or did it?"

Icy little needles pricked my spine. "What do you mean?"

"I mean, Clare *bach*, that despite all the checks we carried out, I was never entirely sure of him. Which is why I went to such lengths to cover my tracks and confuse the issue with pseudonyms – though God knows, I finished by confusing the whole lot of us."

At all costs he mustn't be allowed to doubt Philip – not now. I said sharply, "He's retrieving your precious paintings for you – isn't that proof enough?"

"Not necessarily. You see, the shipment was arranged for tonight all along; telling everyone it was tomorrow was the final safeguard. But if it *had* been, what's the betting the boys in blue would have been waiting for us?"

They might well have been, I thought.

"Am I right?" he prompted.

"Of course you're not right; Philip's in it up to his neck, as you well know."

"Then," Bryn continued, as though I hadn't spoken, "when it was suddenly brought forward, he told you to run for help. Didn't he?"

The last two words shot out, making me jump. "No," I denied quickly, "that was entirely my own idea."

"You'd have betrayed him to the police, when you say you love him?"

"He doesn't want anything to do with me, he made that plain enough. He told me to – keep out of his way." That, at least, was true, and my voice broke most convincingly.

"And hell hath no fury?"

I said in a whisper, "What will you do with me?"

"I've been wondering. You've caused me endless trouble, you know. Just think – if you hadn't appeared on the scene, Carol would have received my message – even if belatedly, Philip would have had hers, Morgan would have contacted them both, and all would have gone according to plan. Instead of which, thanks to you, there's been an unholy mix-up. You agree I have a point?"

"I'm sorry," I said ridiculously.

"No matter, we shall prevail, given a bit of luck. As to you, well, the obvious solution would be an accident."

"Like Dick Harvey?" I asked out of a dry throat.

"The archaeologist? Yes, that was unfortunate – especially for him – but in the circumstances, Morgan had no choice. You had your suspicions, did you? I knew you were too sharp for your own good."

Morgan. I remembered the notes which had arrived so opportunely and prevented him from going walking with me.

I said numbly, "But why was Dick found at Pen-y-Coed?"

"To divert attention from the castle, of course. Morgan guessed that was where he was headed and, by a few devious short cuts, managed to get ahead of him on the road.

"He then stopped and flagged Harvey down as he approached – pretending to be surprised it was him. Told him he was on his way to Pen-y-Coed to meet someone, but had developed a flat tyre. Harvey offered to run him over."

I said tightly, "Which kindness Morgan repaid by pushing him off the cliff. After which, I suppose, he jogged back to where he'd left his car and returned to the hotel."

"Precisely."

It hadn't been much of a risk, setting straight off after Dick, because I'd gone into the dining-room, and I was the only one who knew he was supposed to be working. He couldn't have been long back when he knocked on my door and invited me for a drink. How gullible I'd been.

Another swift glance. "Look, it was hellish bad luck, the guy turning up at this juncture and jeopardising everything. In Morgan's defence, he was quite shaken when he phoned to report it. Said he'd rather liked the fellow."

"He'd recovered himself by lunch-time."

Bryn brushed that aside. "Anyway, we were talking about you. You've got spunk, Clare Laurie, I'll say that for you, and spunk is something I admire."

I was still thinking of poor, kind Dick and his violent end, but a quality in Bryn's soft voice reclaimed my attention.

"Added to which," he went on, "I've always had a weakness for pretty girls, and you are pretty, aren't you? I could tell that by the light of the headlamps, even when you were scared out of your wits."

I moistened parched lips. "So?"

"So I offer you an alternative. More than you deserve, perhaps, but it seems such a waste to kill you."

"And – what is the alternative?"

He was silent for a moment, and I turned to look at him. His mouth was twisted into a smile, as though at some secret joke.

"Marry me," he said.

"*Marry* you?" My voice squeaked on a note of incredulity.

"It's not such a ludicrous idea, you know. You'd be a valuable asset as a wife; your respectability would silence any whispers, and your uncle, as you'll appreciate, would be a powerful ally. A charming man, I thought." He smiled again, and even in this headlong flight, with all our futures dependent on the next half-hour, his voice took on a caressing note.

"Added to which, *cariad*, I should very much enjoy making love to you."

He was mad – he must be! I closed my eyes on a wave of

panic, but his next words proved there was, after all, method in that madness.

"There's also, of course, the small point about a wife's evidence being inadmissible. On the down side, Carol wouldn't be too chuffed, but I'm sure we could accommodate her.

"So – the choice is yours. It's a funny thing, you know: up to now, I've always been on the receiving end of proposals. This is the first I've made myself."

"Thank you," I said, since it seemed expected of me. In the mirror there was no longer any sign of the following car. Bryn's foot was hard down and we continued to rush along like the night wind itself. I presumed we were heading for Swansea, though I'd seen no signposts; he obviously knew the way blindfold. The road was narrower now, and I hoped fearfully that we wouldn't meet any oncoming traffic.

"Do I take it that's an acceptance?"

"I have no choice."

"On the contrary, as I explained."

But the alternatives were equally unreal – Bryn's wife, or a swift push off a cliff. Quite literally, the devil or the deep.

We flashed through the single street of a village. There were lights in the windows, and I realised with a sense of shock that it must still be only about eleven. Twelve hours ago, I'd been reading by the brook.

The ship sailed, Morgan had said, at midnight. They couldn't be far behind. And what of the car in which I'd pinned so much hope? Just a family returning late, who had turned into their own drive?

Bryn jammed on the brakes and my seatbelt jerked me backwards, ricking my neck and knocking the breath out of me.

"Bloody hell!" He swerved up on to the grass bordering the road and skidded to a halt.

"What is it?" I asked, when I could speak.

"They're ahead of us – didn't you just see their lights go out? I never dreamed they'd use the short cut on a night like this. Quickly, get out!"

He switched off our own lights and leapt round the car, dragging me out into the wet darkness. My wrenched ankle buckled under me and I gave a cry, which Bryn ignored.

"I was counting on him thinking I'd make for the motorway," he said, his mouth close to my ear so I could hear above the noise of the elements. "Now, not only has he cut us off, but if Morgan and Carol come this way – or anyone else, for that matter – they'll run straight into him. We'll have to shift him somehow."

He pushed me ahead of him, and we started to run, heads bent, into the wind, cutting across a field so that, as we rounded the corner, we wouldn't be spotted by the reception party awaiting us.

"He'll be out of the car, watching for us. I've a gun here, and if you make a run for it or try to warn him, I promise you I shall use it – on both of you."

I did not doubt him. Shivering in the cold after the humid car, I limped along beside him till he came to a halt, putting out an arm to stop me.

"Down there, look! Two of them, dammit!"

I peered down the slight incline to the road. Sure enough, behind the parked car two figures crouched tensely, one on either side. Bryn said, "Think you can hit one of them?"

I stared at him in horror, numbly shaking my head.

"Well, remember what I said about any warning. If I can creep up on them I'll knock them out, but if they spot me, I'll have to shoot them."

His words were so much a part of this horrific night that they came as no shock. It seemed, after all, quite logical. Stealthily, we circled the unsuspecting figures. Then Bryn gave my arm a last, warning squeeze and crept forward with the reversed gun in his hand.

Praying, for their sakes, that they wouldn't hear him, I moved silently after him. The first figure fell without a sound and he inched to the far side of the car out of my sight. The noise of the wind was in his favour. A moment later I heard him call softly, "Give me a hand to drag them clear. They'll be out for quite a while, by the look of them."

I slithered down on to the hard surface, my eyes fixed on the prone body nearest to me. Without ceremony Bryn rolled it over with his shoe and I gave a startled exclamation. I was looking at the white face of Cindy Dacombe.

"Well, what do you know, another blonde!" Bryn said. "The place is moving with them! Take her feet, and hurry."

I lifted the slim legs in their faded jeans while Bryn took her shoulders. On the verge he dropped her none too gently and we went back for Andrew, who was considerably more cumbersome to move. The red-brown hair was plastered down with rain, and there was an ugly dark stain spreading over his left temple.

"He is all right, isn't he?" I asked fearfully, staggering under his weight.

"He's all right." Bryn's voice was grim. We dumped him beside Cindy and, rubbing my sore arms, I looked in bewilderment from one unconscious face to the other. Their presence here was yet another puzzle.

I jumped as the engine started up beside me. Bryn opened the door. "Get in – no point in going back for my car."

I scrambled in beside him and had barely slammed the door before he'd reversed expertly in the narrow road and started once more in the direction of Swansea.

"You know them, then?" His voice was uneven and he was still breathing heavily.

"Yes, they're a honeymoon couple from the hotel." I spoke absently, my mind elsewhere. Something he'd said earlier . . . "Bryn!" I spoke sharply.

"Yes, *cariad*?"

"You said – Morgan and Carol would have run into them."

"Well?"

"What about Philip? He'll be with them, won't he?"

"The old sixth sense, is it? Well now, it depends, see. If he tried to cause trouble, they might have had to dispose of him."

164

"*Dispose* of him?" I heard the raw horror in my voice.

"That was the arrangement. You see, Clare, I'm coming to the conclusion it was all a put-up job, starting right back with that antiques theft. One hell of an act, with the sole aim of putting paid to my operations. And my God, I just about fell for it! That's a bitter pill, Clare; I don't like being taken for a ride.

"Mind, I set little traps for him from the start, but he always skirted round them. So when I needed a US buyer and couldn't go over there myself, I made that the final test. If Philip carried it off, I'd stop worrying. And I have to tell you he was fantastic, even talking the Yank into agreeing to my price. Couldn't have done better myself, and that's the truth. So, to some extent, I relaxed my guard.

"But Beanstalk was the big one, and it was always going to be tricky. As it turned out, it was a bonus that Philip was expendable; if things went wrong, he could be jettisoned. Even if he talked, it would be his word against mine, and though I'm looked at askance in some quarters, I'm still a reasonably respected art dealer. Whereas his reputation, as you well know, has been publicly shot to hell."

I daren't let myself believe it – not yet – and I shook my head decidedly. "You're wrong; I'm quite certain you can trust him."

"You surprise me," Bryn said drily. "You didn't trust him yourself, did you, three months ago? In fact, you couldn't wait to get rid of him."

Agonisingly, I knew this to be true, as Philip must also have known.

To change a suddenly painful subject, I said with an effort, "Where are we going?"

"To rendezvous with Morgan at the docks. Once the cargo's safely stowed, you and I go straight back to London. As far as anyone knows, I've never left it."

"And you think you can force me to marry you against my will?"

"Not against your will, *cariad* – you'll be only too willing.

Because if you decline, not only will you meet with an accident yourself, but so will your precious Philip – if he hasn't already. If I were you, I'd forget him; he's said he doesn't want you. He'll just assume you were 'one of my girls' after all."

I sat watching the black countryside rush past on either side of us. If Bryn was right, and the whole thing was a frame-up, surely they could have trusted me? Or had Philip simply handed me what he knew I was looking for – the 'perfect excuse' to finish with him?

I remembered Matthew's insistence that Philip needed me, and was sick with shame at my betrayal. As Bryn said, I'd been only too ready to believe the worst of Philip, and Matthew knew how much his ruse was costing him. No wonder he no longer wanted me.

Beside me, Bryn spoke softly. The word was an obscenity. I turned questioningly to look at him.

"I see now why they had to cut us off: the god-damned tank's empty."

"Empty?" My mind still on Philip, I didn't take in what he said.

"No petrol," said Bryn succinctly. "It's showing empty now, God knows how much longer we can keep going. Part of the way's downhill, which will help, but in this head wind I don't think she'll cruise fast enough."

"How much farther is it?"

"Far enough – we won't make it."

Confirming his words, the engine spluttered, choked and died. Bryn stopped, his hands still on the wheel. And through the roaring of wind and crashing of water, a new note reached us – the hysterical, monotonous braying of a police car.

"There's a night we are having, isn't it?" Bryn said with a heavy accent. "Everybody out!"

Wearily I stood once more on the narrow, wetly glinting road. The police cars were not yet in sight, but the sirens were growing louder. I was confused; who had sent for them? Had my desperation reached out to them telepathically?

166

Such musings were cut short as Bryn seized my arm. "Up on the cliffs," he directed. "We haven't time to hide the car – it would need pushing, in any case. Just remember, my lovely, I have a gun." And he gently nudged me with its obscene black muzzle.

Mechanically I turned off the road and with automatic obedience, stumbled after him into the dripping bracken.

Chapter Sixteen

'Chaos of thought and passion, all confused;'
                              Pope: *An Essay on Man*

IT WAS a nightmare journey. My wrenched ankle, by now sending acute shafts of pain up my leg, was causing me considerable discomfort, not helped by Bryn's instruction that we run bent double, to avoid presenting a silhouette against the skyline.

He was keeping firm hold on me, and my other hand, at his insistence, held tightly on to my hood lest the wind drag it off and my fair hair signal our whereabouts.

The bracken through which we were ploughing was in places waist-high and drenched with rain. My jeans were soon soaked, cold and clammy against my legs, and the stitch which I'd had earlier returned to plague me.

Choking, gasping for breath, with no free hand to brush the hair out of my eyes, I stumbled on in a cocoon of misery. I had no thought to spare for the police, conscious only of the need to keep going, of Bryn's stooping figure ahead of me and his occasional oath as a frond of moisture-laden bracken snapped back in his face.

Then it seemed the slope eased off a little, and as it levelled out, I saw we were on the cliffs. Immediately the wind lashed against us, forcing itself into eyes, nose and mouth and robbing us of what little breath we had.

"Over here!" Bryn directed. "There are gorse bushes – they'll provide some cover." Without thought I stumbled after him, gasping and sobbing with pain. Below us on the road the braying grew louder and ceased suddenly with a scream of brakes. They'd found the car.

Voices reached us, calling to one another above the wind. Then, suddenly, light flooded over the lower slopes as headlamps were angled to illuminate the hillside. We, however, were already beyond their reach.

Down on the road, as on to a floodlit stage, half a dozen figures spilled out of the cars and started after us, torches flowering in the dark. Bryn pulled me sharply down, and we crouched, panting, in the undergrowth while the probing fingers of light raked the hillside.

The rain was easing off at last and, as though assisting the search, clouds chased across the sky to reveal the pale disc of the moon.

"There are caves all along here," Bryn said in my ear. "If we can reach one, we'll be safe. But remember, my little bride, I shan't hesitate to shoot if I have to."

He half pushed, half dragged me nearer the cliff edge, but that final spurt proved a mistake. He'd miscalculated the speed of our pursuers, and already the first heads were appearing over the bracken. There was a shout as someone caught sight of us and then, incredibly, Philip's voice:

"By God, he *has* got her!"

My sob was compounded equally of terror and relief that he was alive, but it was choked back as Bryn's hand came roughly over my mouth. Then, seeing further concealment was pointless, he stood up, dragging me in front of him and shouting, "Don't come any closer! I have a gun, and if you force me to use it, Clare goes over the cliff!"

Philip, erupting out of the bracken, stopped dead. I could see him braced against the wind, presenting, to my petrified eyes, an irresistible target. Behind him more figures had appeared, but he held out an arm to keep them back. In the distance another police siren wailed.

Philip cupped his hands round his mouth and shouted back: "Send Clare down, then we can talk."

Bryn laughed excitedly. "Nothing to talk about, boyo, and Clare stays with me."

"Don't be a bloody fool!" Even through the wind I could hear the frustrated anger in Philip's voice. "Rees and Carol are in custody and the police have the paintings."

"Nothing to lose, then, have I?"

Below us on the road, the third police car screeched to a halt. There were more bangings of doors, more voices shouting.

Philip had turned away and appeared to be consulting with the policemen. Barely twenty yards separated us, but with Bryn's gun unwavering in his hand, it could have been twenty miles. I wondered hopelessly how this would end; if Philip came any closer – or, for that matter, any of the other men – I didn't doubt that Bryn would fire. And, I remembered shudderingly, he had sworn to push me over the cliff. We were only a few feet from the edge, and a sonorous booming filled my ears. It didn't take much imagination to picture the huge rocks close under the cliffs and the boiling sea crashing over them.

Bryn was still using me as a shield. Leaning helplessly against him, I could feel the vibration of his heartbeats and his ragged breathing in my ear, and wondered detachedly how long my shaking legs would support me.

Then I felt him stiffen and in the same movement spin round, pulling me with him, and I saw what had alerted him – a crouched figure closing in on us from our left. In the same instant Philip yelled, "*Down*, Clare!" and before his voice had died, I'd twisted free and was flat on the wet, prickly scrub, rolling frantically away from Bryn's feet.

In the same heart-stopping instant, Philip, avoiding the restraining hand of a policeman, hurled himself forward. Bryn fired, but he must have missed because Philip's momentum still carried him onwards, and before he'd a chance of another shot Philip was on to him.

My view of the struggle was temporarily, maddeningly,

blocked as the man who had caused the diversion hauled me to my feet and shoved me unceremoniously behind a gorse bush. From its cover I continued to gaze, horrified, at the grappling bodies swaying crazily together on the cliff edge, outlined against the paler darkness of the sky.

A voice somewhere ahead of me shouted irritably, "What the devil are you waiting for? Close in, before he can draw!"

But even as figures started obediently forward, Bryn, with a strength born of desperation, wrenched himself free and his fist caught Philip's jaw with the impact of a sledgehammer. Off balance, Philip reeled backwards, and instantly, in the fitful light, came the gleam of Bryn's gun.

My eyes strained agonisingly to see how Philip fared. I was hoping the blow had knocked him out and would keep him clear of trouble, but that hope was short-lived. He moved painfully and started to push himself up again. I heard someone shout, "Stay *down*, man!" but he took no notice.

Instinctively, I was on my feet, my throbbing ankle forgotten. I was to Bryn's left now, and slightly behind him, and could see the iron discipline which, though his breathing tore through his body like sobs, kept the gun he held as still as a rock. Every ounce of his concentration was on Philip who, now on hands and knees, paused before the final effort of pushing himself to his feet.

I looked wildly round, but there was no one near me, the man who'd helped me having rejoined his colleagues. I was the only one temporarily out of Bryn's sights. Thankfully there was no time for fear – that had all been spent. Almost coolly, my eyes measured the distance between my bush and Bryn. Fifteen feet at most.

Moving as fluidly as the clouds across the heavens, I slipped out of my cover, my eyes riveted on the figure against the skyline. If he caught any hint of movement, he'd turn and fire. His nerves were stretched to breaking point, but still he watched Philip, waiting for him to stand and present a better target.

As I paused fractionally, I could hear Philip's grunt of exertion, almost feel the flex of his muscles as he came upright. And in that instant I hurled myself forward, low down to avoid the gaping muzzle, and more by the grace of God than any expert manoeuvring on my part, my outflung arms caught Bryn round the knees.

I heard his staccato oath and simultaneously there was a skull-splitting roar, a searing smell of cordite, and the rib-cracking weight of his heavy body falling across mine.

Time had ceased to exist. When Bryn fell on top of me, the force of his body expelling my breath, I lost consciousness for the first time in my life. The three days of strain, with very little sleep to separate them, had finally caught up with me and I slid helplessly into darkness, convinced that the bullet had found its mark in Philip.

Several times over the next hour or so, I swam up briefly to the surface of awareness before drifting away again. During those times, there was a dream-like fluidity about everything around me. As though in another dimension was the smell of petrol and leather and wet clothes, a sensation of moving smoothly and without effort on my part, of voices, sharp with command but quite unintelligble.

Then, eternities later, the motion ceased, cold night wind rushed at me, and I was carried from the warm cocoon of the police car into the familiar hallway of the Carreg Coed hotel. And, in the confusing way of dreams, Matthew was there, his face white with strain, his voice cracking as he cried, "Clare! My God, she's not hurt?"

I obligingly passed out again, and the next thing I remember is being propped up on the sofa in the lounge, wrapped in blankets, while Mrs Davies, wearing an old blue dressing-gown and with her hair in a net, spoon-fed me hot soup. Matthew, who must be real after all, sat next to her, holding my hand.

My instinctive movement brought a twinge from my swollen

172

foot, and I saw it had been expertly bandaged. Its throbbing had underlain all my troubled dreams.

The soup finished amid murmurs of encouragement, Mrs Davies quietly left the room and I felt a flutter of panic; return to full consciousness could no longer be delayed, and I'd been clinging to unreality as an amulet against what I dreaded to hear. For in all the comings and goings, the driftings and dreamings, there had been no sight nor sound of Philip.

It was no use, though; I had to know.

"Philip?" It was the first word I'd spoken, and it came out blurred and indistinct, but Matthew caught it.

"He's all right, Clare. He's giving a statement in another room."

The tide of relief sapped all my energy and it was minutes before I could speak again. Then, as memory began to return, I said urgently, "And the Dacombes?"

"All right too. They're being kept in hospital overnight because of their concussion, but they should be out in the morning." He smiled. "There was talk of carting you off with them, but once it was established your ankle was only sprained, Philip talked them into bringing you back here."

The soup had revived me, and my curiosity returned.

"But what were they *doing* out there?"

He grimaced. "Not much good, as it turned out, though not for want of trying."

"But—"

"They were the undercover we'd arranged."

"Police?" I looked at him in bewilderment. "Then they're not—?"

"Yes, it really is their honeymoon, but as this operation was coming to the boil, I gather their Chief asked if they'd mind combining business with pleasure."

"Good heavens! So how much did they know of what was going on?"

"Philip was keeping them briefed."

"Philip?"

He bit his lip, obviously having let slip more than he'd intended.

I said quietly, "After all this, don't you think I'm entitled to an explanation?"

"It's a long story, Clare, and I promised Philip—"

"I don't want to see him," I interrupted.

He was safe, that was all that mattered. I was not strong enough to listen to his carefully composed expressions of regret, to see his eyes slide evasively from mine.

Matthew said gently, "Everything will be explained in the morning. Now, my dear, you're going to bed. Do you realise it's after one o'clock?"

But I'd no intention of being placated. "Please," I insisted, "whenever and whatever it is, I want you to tell me. Don't make me see Philip."

Behind me the door rocked open, and the voice I'd thought never to hear again demanded tensely, "Has she come round?"

I stiffened, clinging to Matthew's hand, but he extracted it with a little pat and rose to his feet. As the door closed behind him, Philip came quickly round the corner of my vision. His face was white, still spattered with mud, with a streak of blood down one cheek, and his jaw where Bryn's fist had caught him was bruised and swollen. He sat down and took both my hands tightly in his.

"Clare," he said. "Thank God you're safe."

I sat without moving, drained of emotion.

"Darling, I know you're exhausted, but this can't wait – I have to explain why I was so brutal yesterday."

He paused, and I felt him look at me, but was incapable of meeting his eyes.

"You see, the risks hadn't mattered before, when I'd nothing to lose. Then, unbelievably, just when the danger was greatest, it suddenly seemed I'd everything to live for.

"I don't think you realised how desperate it all was; it was quite on the cards that I wouldn't come out of it. Bryn never completely trusted me, I knew that. If you had to be hurt, it seemed preferable for it to be then, before anything had a chance to develop."

Again he paused and again I remained silent.

"Also, it was going to be hard enough for you to extricate yourself from Morgan when Carol arrived, without having you as worried for my safety as I was for yours."

He raised my hands and held them against his cheek. "God, Clare, it was the hardest thing I've ever had to do. Imagine how I felt; after loving you all these years, just when it seemed you might feel the same, I had to push you away."

The lump of ice inside me was beginning to dissolve. He turned my hands over and kissed the palms, one after the other.

"I shouldn't be burdening you with all this now, but I had to explain, try to make you understand. Now, I've kept you long enough; Mrs Davies is waiting for you, so let me help you upstairs."

I had still not said a word, but he didn't seem to expect one. He helped me up, supporting me so that my injured foot was off the floor, and we slowly progressed into the hall. The staircase had never seemed so long, and my legs felt like rubber.

At my door, Philip handed me into Mrs Davies's care and she helped me to undress and slide into bed, where comforting hot-water bottles awaited me.

Then it was dark and my eyes closed of their own volition and I slept as never before.

Chapter Seventeen

'O! wonderful, wonderful, and most wonderful
wonderful!'

Shakespeare: *As You Like It*

I WOKE slowly to the sound of the bedroom curtains being
swished back and the titillating smell of buttered toast and
coffee. The events of the past night rose like bubbles to the
level of consciousness, and I thought with relief – at last, it's
almost over. Almost: but despite his words last night, there was
still a barrier between Philip and me, the reserve which only a
frank and full discussion could dispel.

It was Mrs Davies, not Mair, who stood smiling down at me.
I blinked up at her.

"What time is it?"

"Almost twelve – you've had a good sleep."

"Twelve!" I struggled up in the bed, looking at the clock for
verification. "The day's half gone!"

She laughed. "You had more than your share of yesterday, and you've been well out of it, I can tell you. We've
had quite a time trying to explain things to the guests. The
sudden departure of the Zimmermans, following on the disappearance of Mr Rees and Miss Lawrence, to say nothing
of Mr Hardy's swollen jaw – it was really too much for
them."

I said with a clutch of apprehension, "What happened to
Bryn, do you know?"

"The ringleader? In Swansea jail, with the rest of them."

"He wasn't hurt, then?"

"Not that I know of."

I relaxed, glad that the confrontation which could have ended so disastrously had in fact produced no fatalities. Added to which, as I admitted ruefully to myself, unprincipled and ruthless though he was, Bryn undeniably had charm.

Mrs Davies moved to the door. "Mr Bennett would like a word, when you're ready."

"Of course – please ask him to come in. Perhaps he'd like some coffee."

"I suggested it, but he said it's almost lunch-time. I'll tell him you're awake."

There were dark rings under Matthew's eyes, but his mouth had lost the tightly-drawn tension of last night.

"And how are you this morning?" He bent to kiss me. "Or perhaps I should say, this afternoon?"

"I'm fine," I said.

"And the ankle?"

"I haven't tested it, but it feels a little easier."

"It's amazing you've escaped with nothing worse, after all you've been through. And, heaven help me, I sent you away for a holiday!"

"Seeing you and Philip together is better than any holiday." My voice shook. It seemed my control was more precarious than I'd realised. He took my hand.

"There's a lot for you to forgive, Clare; I hope you feel the ends justify it. Still, Philip insists that all the explanations come from him; he's planning to take you out for the day. I did say you should be resting that foot, but Mrs Davies has unearthed an old walking stick, which at least will help keep your weight off it."

I adroitly changed the subject. "You never explained your miraculous appearance on the scene?"

"It was thanks to your postcard; I nearly had a stroke when it arrived yesterday. Clearly it had been written before Philip showed up, but I knew you must have met during the weekend, just as things were coming to a climax.

"I phoned here immediately, but neither of you could be found and it wasn't the kind of message I could leave with anyone. So I threw a few things into a case and hotfooted it after you.

"I couldn't just suddenly turn up here, though – it might have endangered the whole operation – so I stopped off at the Plas Dinas. I phoned again from there, shortly before six; this time it was the chambermaid who answered. She said you were both out but she'd see you got the message to ring me. Obviously, you didn't. But I wasn't aware of the urgency, or I'd have kept phoning; like Philip, I still thought the action was due to take place tonight."

"How did you hear of the change of plan?"

"Young Dacombe phoned me at home, and Mrs Withers gave him the Plas Dinas number, which I'd left with her. He rang about nine, explained he was the police watchdog we'd arranged, and admitted he was worried; Philip had disappeared and there was no sign of you, Rees or the Lawrence girl. He'd alerted the local police and was about to set off for the castle.

"I was all for going with him but he wouldn't hear of it. I suppose he was right – I'm a bit long in the tooth for cops and robbers. So I came on here, not knowing what on earth was happening and out of my mind with worry for you both."

"Well, fortunately we survived." I wiped the butter off my fingers. "And now I suppose I'd better get up, if Philip's waiting for me."

"He's been waiting for you a long time, Clare."

I didn't encounter anyone on my way downstairs, but I could see Philip's car drawn up outside. He was leaning against it, staring up the hillside where I'd climbed with Clive my first morning.

He turned as he heard my halting footsteps, and came to help me. "How are you this morning?"

"Not too bad, considering, thanks to the improvised crutch. I must say that's a magnificent bruise you have there."

He smiled fleetingly. "Will you come for a drive? We need to talk, don't we?"

I nodded and he took my stick and helped me into the car. It was a day similar to yesterday, a pale blue sky with ragged clouds blowing across the sun. I wished the explanations were behind us and we could be natural with each other.

"The Mortimers and the schoolmarms are to be given a brief resumé after lunch," he said, breaking the silence. I made an effort to help him out.

"What about the old ladies? Are they still there?"

"Oh yes, they were only on the fringe – I'm sure they never realised what Bryn was up to. He'd used them before, but only to listen and report anything that might prove lucrative. He used to tell them it was to help his business. Euphemistic, or what?"

We came to the corner where the road branched left towards the coast and the castle. Philip took the right-hand turn and we started to climb. Far below us at the foot of the valley, a toy-like train scuttled importantly along the silver track, a curl of smoke blowing over its back like a tiny medieval dragon.

We climbed continuously for several miles, the road twisting and turning past the odd stone cottage and isolated farm. Then there were no more buildings, just the grass and the sky. We might have been on the top of the world. Philip steered the car on to the turf and stopped. The silence was complete.

"Can you manage to walk a little way?" he asked. "We won't go far."

I nodded. He helped me out and, with him supporting me on one side and the stick on the other, we moved slowly up a small incline away from the road. The view was panoramic: sweep after sweep of fields, the silver skein of streams threading between them, and clusters of houses nestling in the valley. At intervals, clumps of sheep were bunched together like blobs of icing on the grass, and immediately below us a copse waved scarlet and copper banners against the grey rock.

179

A stone wall ran zigzagging beside us, before giving up farther along in a heap of stones. Everything smelt fresh and newly washed after last night's storm and it was very still. A lark was singing somewhere, and in the distance a dog barked once.

Philip spread his mac on the grass and with his assistance I lowered myself on to it. The wall was at our backs and all Wales spread before us. My mouth was dry. Now, I thought, he can't put it off any longer.

He leant forward, his hands clasped round his knees, not looking at me. "I don't know how much you took in of what I said last night – I know I wasn't very coherent. Did you get the gist of it?"

"I think so."

"That's the most important part, but I'll go back to the beginning and then perhaps you'll see what I was up against. And it's further back than you might think, because I actually met Bryn a year or two ago, at Plas Dinas."

"Yes, he told me."

Philip glanced back over his shoulder, hesitated as though about to say something, then, instead, continued. "We went fishing together, and I must say I enjoyed his company. He was interesting and amusing to be with – and, having grown up hereabouts, knew the best pubs to go to, which was another advantage! During those two days we covered all kinds of topics, among them, our jobs; he told me he was an art dealer, and I mentioned that I was in insurance.

"Then the holiday ended, we said our goodbyes, and I never expected to see him again. But you know how it is: once you've met someone, you seem to keep hearing about them in various contexts – like never having heard of a place, and then seeing it mentioned all the time. And sure enough, a few months later his name came up a couple of times in connection with some rather dubious dealing.

"I was surprised, but there are always rumours circulating and I didn't pay too much attention. Until we heard him mentioned in the context of a series of frauds we'd been looking into for years, and it was at that stage that I began to wonder if I could make use of our acquaintance to get at the truth.

"I was reluctant to do it, though – it smacked too much of duplicity – and I didn't make a move until things came to a head with the fire at Portland House."

He turned again to look at me, a smile touching his mouth. "Which, as I obligingly told you, cost us a cool two million. And again, though obviously we'd no proof, it seemed highly likely Bryn Roberts was involved.

"It was at this point that Carol arrived on the scene – a different kettle of fish altogether. Bryn, as I know from personal experience, can be warm, friendly and amusing, even if he uses these traits to his own ends. Carol, on the other hand, has no redeeming features."

I said drily, "You amaze me."

Philip grinned. "All right, she's a looker, I don't deny that, but she's as hard as nails. If she wants something, she goes for it, no matter who gets hurt in the process. She and Bryn met about a year ago, and he fell for her pretty heavily. Before long, they were planning The Big One.

"If you're wondering how I know all this," he added over his shoulder, "she filled me in pretty thoroughly during our day at the castle. Very full of herself, she was. She couldn't have known how illuminating it was.

"Their first move was to get her installed as secretary-cum-bookkeeper to Lord Glendenning, but in view of Bryn's gallery connections and the occasional whispers about him, they kept their association secret.

"So, she settled into her job, quickly made herself indispensable, and became a trusted member of staff. But as the Hunt Ball drew near, she and Bryn began to crystallise their plans.

"The old boy has gout and never goes to the Ball, but the rest of the family does and traditionally the servants are given the evening off, with one exception who stays behind to serve his lordship his supper. You can guess who volunteered last time."

He paused, his eyes following the scroll of an aeroplane across the sky.

"The rest was easy," he continued. "Though the pictures they'd selected were valuable, they were fairly small and easily portable. So when the time came she passed them out to Bryn, set fire to the gallery, and made great play about 'rescuing' a whole pile of other canvases and trying to contain the fire till the brigade arrived. Needless to say, the gallery was completely gutted and Glendenning gave her a handsome cheque in gratitude for the number she'd saved."

"So what aroused your suspicions?" I prompted.

He grimaced. "Insurance men always suspect fires, specially if valuables are involved. But although by now we had Bryn firmly in our sights – and this seemed to be very much his style – there was nothing whatever to connect him with Carol, and he continued to be seen around with his usual harem. As for Carol herself, Lord Glendenning wouldn't hear a word against her, and it did seem that she'd fought hard to save the majority of the collection.

"The cause of the fire was soon established – a cigar butt in a wastepaper basket; which was a clever touch, because it had happened before, when one of the servants had found the basket merrily ablaze. The old boy's a bit absent-minded, and he's very fond of his port.

"They were also careful to take paintings from only one corner of the gallery, thereby backing up her story of not being able to reach them for the flames, and left enough paintings to be found among the ashes to obscure the exact number that were lost.

"Bryn meanwhile had removed them from their frames – which are still missing, by the way – wrapped them as we saw, and shot straight up here to Cefn Fawr, probably even before the fire was out.

"The next development was sheer luck – good for me,

disastrous for them. I was out on business in a little market town not far from Portland House when I saw them together, having a drink in a bar. I knew who she was – there'd been photos in the press after the fire. So I reported back to Matthew, and we dreamed up the Big Split."

"And you never told me." My voice was low.

"No; I accept full blame for that. Matthew was very anxious you should be put in the picture – he hated the whole idea anyway. But I made it a condition that you weren't told."

That hurt. Philip wasn't looking at me; he was still clasping his knees and staring out over the valley, but a nerve jerked at the corner of his mouth, and I knew that for him, too, this was the hardest part.

I moistened my lips. "Are you going to tell me why?"

"Ostensibly, because your reactions would be carefully watched in certain circles, and it was imperative that they should be entirely natural."

"And – unostensibly?"

I saw his knuckles whiten. "It was by way of an escape clause for you."

"Which," I said bitterly, "I seized with both hands."

"Yes."

"You knew I would?"

"I was pretty sure; the writing had been on the wall for months. It occurred to me that you'd met someone else, which was why I fell so readily for your story about Bryn."

"Your story," I corrected him. "I only confirmed what you said."

"I was pretty wound-up anyway by the time I arrived at Carreg Coed," he said grimly, "and when I saw you waiting in the bar—"

He broke off and drew a long, shuddering breath. I wanted to reach out to him, but something kept my hands tightly clasped in my lap.

"So, to go back," I said, more or less steadily, "you leaked the whereabouts of those antiques. Was that true?"

183

"Yes; it had to be, so much hung on it. It's amazing the contacts you can make when you try. Bryn rang me, as we'd hoped, to offer his sympathy, and things went from there. He introduced me to business colleagues, they passed me on to others, and the thing snowballed. But it was all very small-hat at first; they were cagey of me for a long time, and took some convincing that I was in it for as much as I could get.

"I'm still not sure how far Bryn trusted me – I was never given any job which could be traced back to him – but I had undeniably useful contacts.

"So I was sent to the States to find a buyer and I lit on Zimmerman. He's well-known as a private collector who doesn't ask questions about provenance. Consequently he has quite a cache of stolen goods stashed away. He did, however, insist on coming over for a 'holiday' to view what we had on offer before any commitment was made.

"Once the dates were set, Matthew arranged for undercover police to be laid on, and over the last few days all the suspects – including you, though of course he didn't know that – were kept under surveillance. Hence that red car you were so worried about on Sunday."

And possibly, I thought, the fisherman whom I'd come across twice yesterday.

"You could have told me the truth when I said I wasn't involved. That was the second time you didn't trust me."

He said gently, "It wasn't a question of not trusting you, darling; each time I kept things from you, it was for a different reason. The first was because I thought you didn't love me, the second because I hoped you might. But God, Clare, if you'd known what a strain it was! When you asked me not to give you away for Matthew's sake, it was almost more than I could bear. I suddenly saw myself as you must – a ruthless, hardened criminal, capable of anything." He gave a short laugh. "It wasn't a pleasant experience, I can tell you."

"What happened at the castle?"

"Well, the original plan had been that I'd tip Andrew off before we set out. As you probably know by now, he and Cindy were our police contacts – which, though I couldn't tell you, explained his returning to the TV room that night: we used it as our post-box, leaving notes for each other inside the video recorder. No one ever used it."

"You even suggested that Cindy could be 'Cinderella'," I said indignantly.

He shrugged. "At that point you were still the enemy, and I was intent on muddying the waters. Anyway, last night I'd no chance to warn him, which was why I enlisted your help. Fortunately, though, he became alarmed by our absence and reinforcements set out after us."

"Just as well, because I didn't get the chance to phone."

"No; as soon as I'd passed you that note, I regretted it. I was praying you wouldn't go near the cottage because Morgan, spitting mad at losing you in the dark, was hanging round there, thinking that's where you'd make for.

"The police came down the road with their lights off, and the wind and sea were making so much row he didn't hear the car. Before he knew what was happening, he was securely handcuffed in the back of the police car. Then two of the men came round the headland and were waiting for Carol and me when we returned with the loot.

"After which, of course, we came posthaste in search of you. I couldn't think how you'd got so far unless you'd managed to get a lift. Then Carol remarked with great satisfaction that Bryn must have picked you up. That was the first we knew of his being up here.

"We tore along, and sure enough came on his empty car and, just round the corner, the Dacombes lying out cold by the side of the road. It turned out they'd been given the tip-off when Bryn's car was sighted, and were following it at a discreet distance. They even saw him stop to pick you up, but of course didn't know who you were until we rang them on the mobile asking them to look out for you.

"The rest you know. Incidentally, you probably saved my life up there on the cliff, for which I haven't yet thanked you."

"You're welcome," I said facetiously.

There was a brittle silence, which Philip broke by saying quietly, "Was I right, Clare, about you feeling differently now? Are you going to give me another chance?"

I said in a small, choked voice, "I'm surprised you still want me."

He turned then, and the look in his eyes removed for all time any doubts I might have had. But I went on wretchedly, "I can't think why you loved me in the first place. I was silly and shallow and selfish, and when you needed me most, I turned and ran."

"Sweetheart, don't be too hard on yourself. It was partly my fault, anyway; I handled things appallingly badly. Still, it's all behind us now, and it's the future that's important. Will we be spending it together?"

"Oh yes, please!" I said.

They were the last words spoken for a considerable time. We were both very conscious of how close we'd come to losing each other, and that knowledge made our coming together doubly precious.

Much later, Philip raised his head and said with a smile, "I should have known you couldn't be Goldilocks – you were the Sleeping Beauty. All I can say is, thank God you've woken up at last! It certainly felt like a hundred years!"

I lifted a hand to his face, my fingers gentle on the stretched, bruised skin of his jaw. "Even if it had been, it would have been within my rights; this *is* the storybook ending, isn't it?"

Philip reached into his pocket, drew out my engagement ring, and slipped it back on my finger.

"It's the storybook beginning," he said.